TWO MEN AND A BODY

They had come to the windows of the locked room. French windows, which faced the back of the house. Antony couldn't help feeling a thrill of excitement as he followed Cayley's example and put his face close up to the glass. For the first time he wondered if there really *had* been a shot in this mysterious room. It had all seemed so absurd and melodramatic from the other side of the door. But there had been one shot; why should there not be two more?—at the careless fools who were pressing their noses to the panes, and asking for it.

"My God, can you see it?" said Cayley in a shaking voice. "Down there. Look!"

The next moment Antony saw it. A man was lying on the floor at the far end of the room, his back towards them. A man? Or the body of a man?

THE
RED HOUSE
MYSTERY

A. A. Milne

A DELL BOOK

Published by
Dell Publishing Co., Inc.
1 Dag Hammarskjold Plaza
New York, New York 10017

Dell ® TM 681510, Dell Publishing Co., Inc.

ISBN: 0-440-17376-0

Reprinted by arrangement with E. P. Dutton, a division of New American Library

Printed in the United States of America

Two Previous Dell Editions

August 1987

10 9 8 7 6 5 4 3 2 1

WFH

TO JOHN VINE MILNE

My dear Father,

Like all really nice people, you have a weakness for detective stories, and feel that there are not enough of them. So, after all that you have done for me, the least that I can do for you is write you one. Here it is: with more gratitude and affection than I can well put down here.

A. A. M.

CONTENTS

CHAPTER I

MRS. STEVENS IS FRIGHTENED

In the drowsy heat of the summer afternoon the Red House was taking its siesta. There was a lazy murmur of bees in the flower-borders, a gentle cooing of pigeons in the tops of the elms. From distant lawns came the whir of a mowing-machine, that most restful of all country sounds; making ease the sweeter in that it is taken while others are working.

It was the hour when even those whose business it is to attend to the wants of others have a moment or two for themselves. In the housekeeper's room Audrey Stevens, the pretty parlourmaid, re-trimmed her best hat, and talked idly to her aunt, the cook-housekeeper of Mr. Mark Ablett's bachelor home.

"For Joe?" said Mrs. Stevens placidly, her eye on the hat.

Audrey nodded. She took a pin from her mouth, found a place in the hat for it, and said, "He likes a bit of pink."

"I don't say I mind a bit of pink myself," said her aunt. "Joe Turner isn't the only one."

"It isn't everybody's colour," said Audrey, holding the hat out at arm's-length, and regarding it thoughtfully. "Stylish, isn't it?"

"Oh, it'll suit *you* all right, and it would have suited me at your age. A bit too dressy for me now, though wearing better than some other people, I daresay. I was never the one to pretend to be what I wasn't. If I'm fifty-five, I'm fifty-five—that's what *I* say."

"Fifty-eight, isn't it, auntie?"

"I was just giving that as an example," said Mrs. Stevens with great dignity.

Audrey threaded a needle, held her hand out, and looked at her nails critically for a moment, and then began to sew.

"Funny thing that about Mr. Mark's brother. Fancy not seeing your brother for fifteen years." She gave a self-conscious laugh and went on, "Wonder what I should do if I didn't see Joe for fifteen years."

"As I told you all this morning," said her aunt, "I've been here five years, and never heard of a brother. I could say that before everybody if I was going to die to-morrow. There's been no brother here while I've been here."

"You could have knocked me down with a feather when he spoke about him at breakfast this morning. I didn't hear what went before, naturally, but they was all talking about the brother when I went in—now what was it I went in for—hot milk, was it, or toast?—well, they was all talking, and Mr. Mark turns to me, and says—you know his way—'Stevens,' he says, 'my brother is coming to see me this afternoon; I'm expecting him about three,' he says. 'Show him into the office,' just like that. 'Yes, sir,' I says quite quietly, but I was never so surprised in my life, not knowing he had a brother. 'My brother from Australia,' he says —there, I'd forgotten that. From Australia."

"Well, he may have been in Australia," said Mrs. Stevens, judicially; "I can't say for that, not knowing the country; but what I do say is he's never been here. Not while I've been here, and that's five years."

"Well, but, auntie, he hasn't been here for fifteen years. I heard Mr. Mark telling Mr. Cayley. 'Fifteen years,' he says. Mr. Cayley having arst him when his brother was last in England. Mr. Cayley knew of him, I heard him telling Mr. Beverley, but didn't know when he was last in England—see? So that's why he arst Mr. Mark."

"I'm not saying anything about fifteen years, Audrey. I can only speak for what I know, and that's five years Whitsuntide. I can take my oath he's not set foot in the house since five years Whitsuntide. And if he's been in Australia, as you say, well, I daresay he's had his reasons."

"What reasons?" said Audrey lightly.

"Never mind what reasons. Being in the place of a mother to you, since your poor mother died, I say this, Audrey—when a gentleman goes to Australia, he has his reasons. And when he stays in Australia fifteen years, as Mr. Mark says, and as I know for myself for five years, he has his reasons. And a respectably brought-up girl doesn't ask what reasons."

"Got into trouble, I suppose," said Audrey carelessly. "They were saying at breakfast he'd been a wild one. Debts. I'm glad Joe isn't like that. He's got fifteen pounds in the post-office savings' bank. Did I tell you?"

But there was not to be any more talk of Joe Turner that afternoon. The ringing of a bell brought Audrey to her feet—no longer Audrey, but now Stevens. She arranged her cap in front of the glass.

"There, that's the front door," she said. "That's him. 'Show him into the office,' said Mr. Mark. I suppose he doesn't want the other ladies and gentlemen

to see him. Well, they're all out at their golf, anyhow—
Wonder if he's going to stay—P'raps he's brought
back a lot of gold from Australia—I might hear something about Australia, because if *anybody* can get gold
there, then I don't say but what Joe and I——"

"Now, now, get on, Audrey."

"Just going, darling."

She went out.

To anyone who had just walked down the drive **in**
the August sun, the open door of the Red House revealed a delightfully inviting hall, of which even the
mere sight was cooling. It was a big low-roofed, oak-
beamed place, with cream-washed walls and diamond-
paned windows, blue-curtained. On the right and left
were doors leading into other living-rooms, but on the
side which faced you as you came in were windows
again, looking on to a small grass court, and from
open windows to open windows such air as there was
played gently. The staircase went up in broad, low
steps along the right-hand wall, and, turning to the
left, led you along a gallery, which ran across the
width of the hall, to your bedroom. That is, if you
were going to stay the night. Mr. Robert Ablett's intentions in this matter were as yet unknown.

As Audrey came across the hall she gave a little
start as she saw Mr. Cayley suddenly, sitting unob-
trusively in a seat beneath one of the front windows,
reading. No reason why he shouldn't be there; certainly a much cooler place than the golflinks on such
a day; but somehow there was a deserted air about
the house that afternoon, as if all the guests were
outside, or—perhaps the wisest place of all—up in their
bedrooms, sleeping. Mr. Cayley, the master's cousin,
was a surprise; and, having given a little exclama-
tion as she came suddenly upon him, she blushed, and

said, "Oh, I beg your pardon, sir, I didn't see you at first," and he looked up from his book and smiled at her. An attractive smile it was on that big ugly face. "Such a gentleman, Mr. Cayley," she thought to herself as she went on, and wondered what the master would do without him. If this brother, for instance, had to be bundled back to Australia, it was Mr. Cayley who would do most of the bundling.

"So this is Mr. Robert," said Audrey to herself, as she came in sight of the visitor.

She told her aunt afterwards that she would have known him anywhere for Mr. Mark's brother, but she would have said that in any event. Actually she was surprised. Dapper little Mark, with his neat pointed beard and his carefully-curled moustache; with his quick-darting eyes, always moving from one to the other of any company he was in, to register one more smile to his credit when he had said a good thing, one more expectant look when he was only waiting his turn to say it; he was a very different man from this rough-looking, ill-dressed colonial, staring at her so loweringly.

"I want to see Mr. Mark Ablett," he growled. It sounded almost like a threat.

Audrey recovered herself and smiled reassuringly at him. She had a smile for everybody.

"Yes, sir. He is expecting you, if you will come this way."

"Oh! So you know who I am, eh?"

"Mr. Robert Ablett?"

"Ay, that's right. So he's expecting me, eh? He'll be glad to see me, eh?"

"If you will come this way, sir," said Audrey primly.

She went to the second door on the left, and opened it.

"Mr. Robert Ab——" she began, and then broke off. The room was empty. She turned to the man behind her. "If you will sit down, sir, I will find the master. I know he's in, because he told me that you were coming this afternoon."

"Oh!" He looked round the room. "What d'you call this place, eh?"

"The office, sir."

"The office?"

"The room where the master works, sir."

"Works, eh? That's new. Didn't know he'd ever done a stroke of work in his life."

"Where he *writes*, sir," said Audrey, with dignity. The fact that Mr. Mark "wrote," though nobody knew what, was a matter of pride in the house-keeper's room.

"Not well-dressed enough for the drawing-room, eh?"

"I will tell the master you are here, sir," said Audrey decisively.

She closed the door and left him there.

Well! Here was something to tell auntie! Her mind was busy at once, going over all the things which he had said to her and she had said to him—quiet-like. "Directly I saw him I said to myself——" Why, you could have knocked her over with a feather. Feathers, indeed, were a perpetual menace to Audrey.

However, the immediate business was to find the master. She walked across the hall to the library, glanced in, came back a little uncertainly, and stood in front of Cayley.

"If you please, sir," she said in a low, respectful

voice, "can you tell me where the master is? It's Mr. Robert called."

"What?" said Cayley, looking up from his book. "Who?"

Audrey repeated her question.

"I don't know. Isn't he in the office? He went up to the Temple after lunch. I don't think I've seen him since."

"Thank you, sir. I will go up to the Temple."

Cayley returned to his book.

The "Temple" was a brick summer-house, in the gardens at the back of the house, about three hundred yards away. Here Mark meditated sometimes before retiring to the "office" to put his thoughts upon paper. The thoughts were not of any great value; moreover, they were given off at the dinner-table more often than they got on to paper, and got on to paper more often than they got into print. But that did not prevent the master of the Red House from being a little pained when a visitor treated the Temple carelessly, as if it had been erected for the ordinary purposes of flirtation and cigarette-smoking. There had been an occasion when two of his guests had been found playing fives in it. Mark had said nothing at the time, save to ask—with a little less than his usual point—whether they couldn't find anywhere else for their game, but the offenders were never asked to the Red House again.

Audrey walked slowly up to the Temple, looked in and walked slowly back. All that walk for nothing. Perhaps the master was upstairs in his room. "Not well-dressed enough for the drawing-room." Well, now, Auntie, would *you* like anyone in *your* drawing-room with a red handkerchief round his neck and great big dusty boots, and—listen! One of the men shooting rabbits. Auntie was partial to a nice rabbit and onion sauce. How hot it was; she wouldn't say no to a cup of tea. Well, one thing, Mr. Robert wasn't staying the night; he hadn't any luggage. Of course Mr. Mark could lend him things; he had clothes for six. She would have known him anywhere for Mr. Mark's brother.

She came into the house. As she passed the housekeeper's room on her way to the hall, the door opened suddenly, and a rather frightened face looked out.

"Hallo, Aud," said Elsie. "It's Audrey," she said, turning into the room.

"Come in, Audrey," called Mrs. Stevens.

"What's up?" said Audrey, looking in at the door.

"Oh, my dear, you gave me such a turn. Where have you been?"

"Up to the Temple."

"Did you hear anything?"

"Hear what?"

"Bangs and explosions and terrible things."

"Oh," said Audrey, rather relieved. "One of the men shooting rabbits. Why, I said to myself as I came along, 'Auntie's partial to a nice rabbit,' I said, and I shouldn't be surprised if——"

"Rabbits!" said her aunt scornfully. "It was inside the house, my girl."

"Straight it was," said Elsie. She was one of the housemaids. "I said to Mrs. Stevens—didn't I, Mrs. Stevens?—'That was in the house,' I said."

Audrey looked at her aunt and then at Elsie.

"Do you think he had a revolver with him?" she said in a hushed voice.

"Who?" said Elsie excitedly.

"That brother of his. From Australia. I said as soon as I set eyes on him, 'You're a bad lot, my man!' That's what *I* said, Elsie. Even before he spoke to me. Rude!" She turned to her aunt. "Well, I give you *my* word."

"If you remember, Audrey, I always said there was no saying with anyone from Australia." Mrs. Stevens lay back in her chair, breathing rather rapidly. "I wouldn't go out of this room now, not if you paid me a hundred thousand pounds."

"Oh, Mrs. Stevens!" said Elsie, who badly wanted five shillings for a new pair of shoes, "I wouldn't go as far as that, not myself, but——"

"There!" cried Mrs. Stevens, sitting up with a start.

They listened anxiously, the two girls instinctively coming closer to the older woman's chair.

A door was being shaken, kicked, rattled.

"Listen!"

Audrey and Elsie looked at each other with frightened eyes.

They heard a man's voice, loud, angry.

"Open the door!" it was shouting. "Open the door! I say, open the door!"

"Don't open the door!" cried Mrs. Stevens in a panic, as if it was her door which was threatened. "Audrey! Elsie! Don't let him in!"

"Damn it, open the door," came the voice again.

"We're all going to be murdered in our beds," she quavered. Terrified, the two girls huddled closer, and with an arm round each, Mrs. Stevens sat there, waiting.

CHAPTER II

MR. GILLINGHAM GETS OUT AT THE WRONG STATION

Whether Mark Ablett was a bore or not depended on the point of view, but it may be said at once that he never bored his company on the subject of his early life. However, stories get about. There is always somebody who knows. It was understood—and this, anyhow, on Mark's own authority—that his father had been a country clergyman. It was said that, as a boy, Mark had attracted the notice, and patronage, of some rich old spinster of the neighbourhood, who had paid for his education, both at school and university. At about the time when he was coming down from Cambridge, his father had died; leaving behind him a few debts, as a warning to his family, and a reputation for short sermons, as an example to his successor. Neither warning nor example seems to have been effective. Mark went to London, with an allowance from his patron, and (it is generally agreed) made acquaintance with the money-lenders. He was supposed, by his patron and any others who inquired, to be "writing"; but what he wrote, other than letters asking for more time to pay, has never been discovered. However, he attended the theatres and music halls very regularly—no doubt with a view to some serious articles in the "Spectator" on the decadence of the English stage.

Fortunately (from Mark's point of view) his patron died during his third year in London, and left him all the money he wanted. From that moment his life loses its legendary character, and becomes more a matter of history. He settled accounts with the money-lenders, abandoned his crop of wild oats to the harvesting of others, and became in his turn a patron. He patronized the Arts. It was not only usurers who discovered that Mark Ablett no longer wrote for money; editors were now offered free contributions as well as free lunches; publishers were given agreements for an occasional slender volume, in which the author paid all expenses and waived all royalties; promising young painters and poets dined with him; and he even took a theatrical company on tour, playing host and "lead" with equal lavishness.

He was not what most people call a snob. A snob has been defined carelessly as a man who loves a lord; and, more carefully, as a mean lover of mean things—which would be a little unkind to the peerage if the first definition were true. Mark had his vanities undoubtedly, but he would sooner have met an actor-manager than an earl; he would have spoken of his friendship with Dante—had that been possible —more glibly than of his friendship with the Duke. Call him a snob if you like, but not the worst kind of snob; a hanger-on, but to the skirts of Art, not Society; a climber, but in the neighborhood of Parnassus, not of Hay Hill.

His patronage did not stop at the Arts. It also included Matthew Cayley, a small cousin of thirteen, whose circumstances were as limited as had been Mark's own before his patron had rescued him. He sent the Cayley cousin to school and Cambridge. His motives, no doubt, were unworldly enough at first; a mere repaying to his account in the Recording Angel's book of the generosity which had been lavished on himself; a laying-up of treasure in heaven. But it is probable that, as the boy grew up, Mark's designs for his future were based on his own interests as much as those of his cousin, and that a suitably educated Matthew Cayley of twenty-three was felt by him to be a useful property for a man in his position; a man, that is to say, whose vanities left him so little time for his affairs.

Cayley, then, at twenty-three, looked after his cousin's affairs. By this time Mark had bought the Red House and the considerable amount of land which went with it. Cayley superintended the necessary staff. His duties, indeed, were many. He was not quite secretary, not quite land-agent, not quite business-adviser, not quite companion, but something of all four. Mark leant upon him and called him "Cay," objecting quite rightly in the circumstances to the name of Matthew. Cay, he felt, was, above all, dependable; a big, heavy-jawed, solid fellow, who didn't bother you with unnecessary talk—a boon to a man who liked to do most of the talking himself.

Cayley was now twenty-eight, but had all the appearance of forty, which was his patron's age. Spasmodically they entertained a good deal at the Red House, and Mark's preference—call it kindliness or vanity, as you please—was for guests who were not in a position to repay his hospitality. Let us have a look at them as they came down to that breakfast, of which Stevens, the parlourmaid, has already given us a glimpse.

The first to appear was Major Rumbold, a tall, grey-haired, grey-moustached, silent man, wearing a

Norfolk coat and grey flannel trousers, who lived on
his retired pay and wrote natural history articles for
the papers. He inspected the dishes on the sidetable,
decided carefully on kedgeree, and got to work on it.
He had passed on to a sausage by the time of the next
arrival. This was Bill Beverley, a cheerful young
man in white flannel trousers and a blazer.

"Hallo, Major," he said as he came in, "how's the
gout?"

"It isn't gout," said the Major gruffly.

"Well, whatever it is."

The Major grunted.

"I make a point of being polite at breakfast," said
Bill, helping himself largely to porridge. "Most people are so rude. That's why I asked you. But don't tell
me if it's a secret. Coffee?" he added, as he poured
himself out a cup.

"No, thanks. I never drink till I've finished eat-
ing."

"Quite right, Major; it's only manners." He sat
down opposite to the other. "Well, we've got a good
day for our game. It's going to be dashed hot, but
that's where Betty and I score. On the fifth green,
your old wound, the one you got in that frontier
skirmish in '43, will begin to trouble you; on the
eighth, your liver, undermined by years of curry,
will drop to pieces; on the twelfth——"

"Oh, shut up, you ass!"

"Well, I'm only warning you. Hallo; good morning, Miss Norris. I was just telling the Major what
was going to happen to you and him this morning.
Do you want any assistance, or do you prefer choosing your own breakfast?"

"Please don't get up," said Miss Norris. "I'll help

myself. Good morning, Major." She smiled pleasantly at him.

The Major nodded.

"Good morning. Going to be hot."

"As I was telling him," began Bill, "that's where—— Hallo, here's Betty. Morning, Cayley."

Betty Calladine and Cayley had come in together. Betty was the eighteen-year-old daughter of Mrs. John Calladine, widow of the painter, who was acting hostess on this occasion for Mark. Ruth Norris took herself seriously as an actress and, on her holidays, seriously as a golfer. She was quite competent as either. Neither the Stage Society nor Sandwich had any terrors for her.

"By the way, the car will be round at 10:30," said Cayley, looking up from his letters. "You're lunching there, and driving back directly afterwards. Isn't that right?"

"I don't see why we shouldn't have two rounds," said Bill hopefully.

"Much too hot in the afternoon," said the Major. "Get back comfortably for tea."

Mark came in. He was generally the last. He greeted them and sat down to toast and tea. Breakfast was not his meal. The others chattered gently while he read his letters.

"Good God!" said Mark suddenly.

There was an instinctive turning of heads towards him.

"I beg your pardon, Miss Norris. Sorry, Betty."

Miss Norris smiled her forgiveness. She often wanted to say it herself, particularly at rehearsals.

"I say, Cay!" He was frowning to himself—annoyed, puzzled. He held up a letter and shook it. "Who do you think this is from?"

Cayley, at the other end of the table, shrugged his shoulders. How could he possibly guess?

"Robert," said Mark.

"Robert?" It was difficult to surprise Cayley. "Well?"

"It's all very well to say 'Well?' like that," said Mark peevishly. "He's coming here this afternoon."

"I thought he was in Australia, or somewhere."

"Of course. So did I." He looked across at Rumbold. "Got any brothers, Major?"

"No."

"Well, take my advice, and don't have any."

"Not likely to now," said the Major.

Bill laughed. Miss Norris said politely: "But *you* haven't any brothers, Mr. Ablett?"

"One," said Mark grimly. "If you're back in time you'll see him this afternoon. He'll probably ask you to lend him five pounds. Don't."

Everybody felt a little uncomfortable.

"I've got a brother," said Bill helpfully, "but I always borrow from *him*."

"Like Robert," said Mark.

"When was he in England last?" asked Cayley.

"About fifteen years ago, wasn't it? You'd have been a boy, of course."

"Yes, I remember seeing him once about then, but I didn't know if he had been back since."

"No. Not to my knowledge." Mark, still obviously upset, returned to his letter.

"Personally," said Bill, "I think relations are a great mistake."

"All the same," said Betty a little daringly, "it must be rather fun having a skeleton in the cupboard."

Mark looked up, frowning.

"If you think it's fun, I'll hand him over to you, Betty. If he's anything like he used to be, and like his few letters have been—well, Cay knows."

Cayley grunted.

"All I knew was that one didn't ask questions about him."

It may have been meant as a hint to any too curious guest not to ask more questions, or a reminder to his host not to talk too freely in front of strangers, although he gave it the sound of a mere statement of fact. But the subject dropped, to be succeeded by the more fascinating one of the coming foursome. Mrs. Calladine was driving over with the players in order to lunch with an old friend who lived near the links, and Mark and Cayley were remaining at home—on affairs. Apparently "affairs" were now to include a prodigal brother. But that need not make the foursome less enjoyable.

At about the time when the Major (for whatever reasons) was fluffing his tee-shot at the sixteenth, and Mark and his cousin were at their business at the Red House, an attractive gentleman of the name of Antony Gillingham was handing up his ticket at Woodham station and asking the way to the village. Having received directions, he left his bag with the station-master and walked off leisurely. He is an important person to this story, so that it is as well we should know something about him before letting him loose in it. Let us stop him at the top of the hill on some excuse, and have a good look at him.

The first thing we realize is that he is doing more of the looking than we are. Above a clean-cut, clean-shaven face, of the type usually associated with the Navy, he carries a pair of grey eyes which seem to be absorbing every detail of our person. To strangers this look is almost alarming at first, until they discover that his mind is very often elsewhere; that he has, so to speak, left his eyes on guard, while he himself follows a train of thought in another direction. Many people do this, of course; when, for instance, they are talking to one person and trying to listen to another; but their eyes betray them. Antony's never did.

He had seen a good deal of the world with those eyes, though never as a sailor. When at the age of twenty-one he came into his mother's money, £400 a year, old Gillingham looked up from the "Stock-breeders' Gazette" to ask him what he was going to do.

"See the world," said Antony.

"Well, send me a line from America, or wherever you get to."

"Right," said Antony.

Old Gillingham returned to his paper. Antony was a younger son, and, on the whole, not so interesting to his father as the cadets of certain other families; Champion Birket's, for instance. But, then, Champion Birket was the best Hereford bull he had ever bred.

Antony, however, had no intention of going further away than London. His idea of seeing the world was to see, not countries, but people; and to see them from as many angles as possible. There are all sorts in London if you know how to look at them. So Antony looked at them—from various strange corners; from the view-point of the valet, the newspaper-reporter, the waiter, the shop-assistant. With the independence of £400 a year behind him, he enjoyed it immensely. He never stayed long in one job, and generally closed his connexion with it by telling his employer (contrary to all etiquette as understood between master and servant) exactly what he thought of him. He had no difficulty in finding a new profession. Instead of experience and testimonials he offered his personality and a sporting bet. He would take no wages the first month, and—if he satisfied his employer—double wages the second. He always got his double wages.

He was now thirty. He had come to Woodham for a holiday, because he liked the look of the station. His ticket entitled him to travel further, but he had always intended to please himself in the matter. Woodham attracted him, and he had a suit-case in the carriage with him and money in his pocket. Why not get out?

The landlady of the "George" was only too glad to put him up, and promised that her husband would drive over that afternoon for his luggage.

"And you would like some lunch, I expect, sir."

"Yes, but don't give yourself any trouble about it. Cold anything-you've-got."

"What about beef, sir?" she asked, as if she had a hundred varieties of meat to select from, and was offering him her best.

"That will do splendidly. And a pint of beer."

While he was finishing his lunch, the landlord came in to ask about the luggage. Antony ordered another pint, and soon had him talking.

"It must be rather fun to keep a country inn," he said, thinking that it was about time he started another profession.

"I don't know about fun, sir. It gives us a living, and a bit over."

"You ought to take a holiday," said Antony, looking at him thoughtfully.

"Funny thing your saying that," said the landlord, with a smile. "Another gentleman, over from the Red House, was saying that on'y yesterday. Offered to take my place an all." He laughed rumblingly.

"The Red House? Not the Red House, Stanton?"

"That's right, sir. Stanton's the next station to Woodham. The Red House is about a mile from here—Mr. Ablett's."

Antony took a letter from his pocket. It was addressed from "The Red House, Stanton," and signed "Bill."

"Good old Bill," he murmured to himself. "He's getting on."

Antony had met Bill Beverley two years before in a tobacconist's shop. Gillingham was on one side of the counter and Mr. Beverley on the other. Something about Bill, his youth and freshness, perhaps, attracted Antony; and when cigarettes had been ordered, and an address given to which they were to be sent, he remembered that he had come across an aunt of Beverley's once at a country-house. Beverley and he met again a little later at a restaurant. Both of them were in evening-dress, but they did different things with their napkins, and Antony was the more polite of the two. However, he still liked Bill. So on one of his holidays, when he was unemployed, he arranged an introduction through a mutual friend. Beverley was a little inclined to be shocked when he was reminded of their previous meetings, but his uncomfortable feeling soon wore off, and he and Antony quickly became intimate. But Bill generally addressed him as "Dear Madman" when he happened to write.

Antony decided to stroll over to the Red House after lunch and call upon his friend. Having inspected his bedroom, which was not quite the lavender-smelling country-inn bedroom of fiction, but sufficiently clean and comfortable, he set out over the fields.

As he came down the drive and approached the old red-brick front of the house, there was a lazy murmur of bees in the flower-borders, a gentle cooing of pigeons in the tops of the elms, and from distant lawns the whir of a mowing-machine, that most restful of all country sounds. . . .

And in the hall a man was banging at a locked door, and shouting, "Open the *door*, I say; open the *door!*"

"Hallo!" said Antony in amazement.

CHAPTER III

TWO MEN AND A BODY

Cayley looked round suddenly at the voice. "Can I help?" said Antony politely.

"Something's happened," said Cayley. He was breathing quickly. "I heard a shot—it sounded like a shot—I was in the library. A loud bang—I didn't know what it was. And the door's locked." He rattled the handle again, and shook it. "Open the *door!*" he cried. "I say, Mark, what is it? Open the door!"

"But he must have locked the door on purpose," said Antony. "So why should he open it just because you ask him to?"

Cayley looked at him in a bewildered way. Then he turned to the door again. "We must break it in," he said, putting his shoulder to it. "Help me."

"Isn't there a window?"

Cayley turned to him stupidly.

"Window? Window?"

"So much easier to break in a window," said Antony with a smile. He looked very cool and collected, as he stood just inside the hall, leaning on his stick, and thinking, no doubt, that a great deal of fuss was being made about nothing. But then, he had not heard the shot.

"Window—of course! What an idiot I am."

He pushed past Antony, and began running out

into the drive. Antony followed him. They ran along
the front of the house, down a path to the left, and
then to the left again over the grass, Cayley in front,
the other close behind him. Suddenly Cayley looked
over his shoulder and pulled up short.

"Here," he said.

They had come to the windows of the locked room,
French windows which opened on to the lawns at
the back of the house. But now they were closed.
Antony couldn't help feeling a thrill of excitement
as he followed Cayley's example, and put his face
close up to the glass. For the first time he wondered
if there really *had* been a revolver shot in this mysterious room. It had all seemed so absurd and melodramatic from the other side of the door. But if
there had been one shot, why should there not be
two more?—at the careless fools who were pressing
their noses against the panes, and asking for it.

"My God, can you see it?" said Cayley in a shaking
voice. "Down there. Look!"

The next moment Antony saw it. A man was lying
on the floor at the far end of the room, his back
towards them. A man? Or the body of a man?

"Who is it?" said Antony.

"I don't know," the other whispered.

"Well, we'd better go and see." He considered the
windows for a moment. "I should think, if you put
your weight into it, just where they join, they'll give
all right. Otherwise, we can kick the glass in."

Without saying anything, Cayley put his weight
into it. The window gave, and they went into the
room. Cayley walked quickly to the body, and
dropped on his knees by it. For the moment he
seemed to hesitate; then with an effort he put a hand
onto its shoulder and pulled it over.

"Thank God!" he murmured, and let the body go again.

"Who is it?" said Antony.

"Robert Ablett."

"Oh!" said Antony. "I thought his name was Mark," he added, more to himself than to the other.

"Yes, Mark Ablett lives here. Robert is his brother." He shuddered, and said, "I was afraid it was Mark."

"Was Mark in the room too?"

"Yes," said Cayley absently. Then, as if resenting suddenly these questions from a stranger, "Who are you?"

But Antony had gone to the locked door, and was turning the handle. "I suppose he put the key in his pocket," he said, as he came back to the body again.

"Who?"

Antony shrugged his shoulders.

"Whoever did this," he said, pointing to the man on the floor. "Is he dead?"

"Help me," said Cayley simply.

They turned the body on to its back, nerving themselves to look at it. Robert Ablett had been shot between the eyes. It was not a pleasant sight, and with his horror Antony felt a sudden pity for the man beside him, and a sudden remorse for the careless, easy way in which he had treated the affair. But then one always went about imagining that these things *didn't* happen—except to other people. It was difficult to believe in them just at first, when they happened to yourself.

"Did you know him well?" said Antony quietly. He meant, "Were you fond of him?"

"Hardly at all. Mark is *my* cousin. I mean, Mark is the brother I know best."

"Your cousin?"

"Yes." He hesitated, and then said, "Is he dead? I suppose he is. Will you—do you know anything about—about that sort of thing? Perhaps I'd better get some water."

There was another door opposite to the locked one, which led, as Antony was to discover for himself directly, into a passage from which opened two more rooms. Cayley stepped into the passage, and opened the door on the right. The door from the office, through which he had gone, remained open. The door at the end of the short passage was shut. Antony, kneeling by the body, followed Cayley with his eyes, and, after he had disappeared, kept his eyes on the blank wall of the passage, but he was not conscious of that at which he was looking, for his mind was with the other man, sympathizing with him.

"Not that water is any use to a dead body," he said to himself, "but the feeling that you're doing something, when there's obviously nothing to be done, is a great comfort."

Cayley came into the room again. He had a sponge in one hand, a handkerchief in the other. He looked at Antony. Antony nodded. Cayley murmured something, and knelt down to bathe the dead man's face. Then he placed the handkerchief over it. A little sigh escaped Antony, a sigh of relief.

They stood up and looked at each other.

"If I can be of any help to you," said Antony, "please let me."

"That's very kind of you. There will be things to do. Police, doctors—I don't know. But you mustn't let me trespass on your kindness. Indeed, I should apologise for having trespassed so much already."

"I came to see Beverley. He is an old friend of mine."

"He's out playing golf. He will be back directly." Then, as if he had only just realized it, "They will all be back directly."

"I will stay if I can be of any help."

"Please do. You see, there are women. It will be rather painful. If you would——" He hesitated, and gave Antony a timid little smile, pathetic in so big and self-reliant a man. "Just your moral support, you know. It would be something."

"Of course." Antony smiled back at him, and said cheerfully, "Well, then, I'll begin by suggesting that you should ring up the police."

"The police? Y—yes." He looked doubtfully at the other. "I suppose——"

Antony spoke frankly.

"Now, look here, Mr.—er——"

"Cayley. I'm Mark Ablett's cousin. I live with him."

"My name's Gillingham. I'm sorry, I ought to have told you before. Well now, Mr. Cayley, we shan't do any good by pretending. Here's a man been shot—well, somebody shot him."

"He might have shot himself," mumbled Cayley.

"Yes, he might have, but he didn't. Or if he did, somebody was in the room at the time, and that somebody isn't here now. And that somebody took a revolver away with him. Well, the police will want to say a word about that, won't they?"

Cayley was silent, looking on the ground.

"Oh, I know what you're thinking, and believe me I do sympathize with you, but we can't be children about it. If your cousin Mark Ablett was in the room with this"—he indicated the body—"this man, then——"

"Who said he was?" said Cayley, jerking his head up suddenly at Antony.

"You did."

"I was in the library. Mark went in—he may have come out again—I know nothing. Somebody else may have gone in——"

"Yes, yes," said Antony patiently, as if to a little child. "You know your cousin; I don't. Let's agree that he had nothing to do with it. But somebody was in the room when this man was shot, and—well, the police will have to know. Don't you think——" He looked at the telephone. "Or would you rather I did it?"

Cayley shrugged his shoulders and went to the telephone.

"May I—er—look round a bit?" Antony nodded towards the open door.

"Oh, do. Yes." He sat down and drew the telephone towards him. "You must make allowances for me, Mr. Gillingham. You see, I've known Mark for a very long time. But, of course, you're quite right, and I'm merely being stupid." He took off the receiver.

Let us suppose that, for the purpose of making a first acquaintance with this "office," we are coming into it from the hall, through the door which is now locked, but which, for our special convenience, has been magically unlocked for us. As we stand just inside the door, the length of the room runs right and left; or, more accurately, to the right only, for the left-hand wall is almost within our reach. Immediately opposite to us, across the breadth of the room (some fifteen feet), is that other door, by which

Cayley went out and returned a few minutes ago. In the right-hand wall, thirty feet away from us, are the French windows. Crossing the room and going out by the opposite door, we come into a passage, from which two rooms lead. The one on the right, into which Cayley went, is less than half the length of the office, a small, square room, which has evidently been used some time or other as a bedroom. The bed is no longer there, but there is a basin, with hot and cold taps, in a corner; chairs; a cupboard or two, and a chest of drawers. The window faces the same way as the French windows in the next room; but anybody looking out of the bedroom window has his view on the immediate right shut off by the outer wall of the office, which projects, by reason of its greater length, fifteen feet further into the lawn.

The room on the other side of the bedroom is a bathroom. The three rooms together, in fact, form a sort of private suite; used, perhaps, during the occupation of the previous owner, by some invalid, who could not manage the stairs, but allowed by Mark to fall into disuse, save for the living-room. At any rate, he never slept downstairs.

Antony glanced at the bathroom, and then wandered into the bedroom, the room into which Cayley had been. The window was open, and he looked out at the well-kept grass beneath him, and the peaceful stretch of park beyond; and he felt very sorry for the owner of it all, who was now mixed up in so grim a business.

"Cayley thinks he did it," said Antony to himself. "That's obvious. It explains why he wasted so much time banging on the door. Why should he try to break a lock when it's so much easier to break a window? Of course he might just have lost his head;

on the other hand, he might—well, he might have
wanted to give his cousin a chance of getting away.
The same about the police, and—oh, lots of things.
Why, for instance, did we run all the way round the
house in order to get to the windows? Surely there's
a back way out through the hall. I must have a look
later on."

Antony, it will be observed, had by no means lost
his head.

There was a step in the passage outside, and he
turned round, to see Cayley in the doorway. He
remained looking at him for a moment, asking himself a question. It was rather a curious question. He
was asking himself why the door was open.

Well, not exactly why the door was open; that
could be explained easily enough. But why had he
expected the door to be shut. He did not remember
shutting it, but somehow he was surprised to see it
open now, to see Cayley through the doorway, just
coming into the room. Something working subconsciously in his brain had told him that it was surprising. Why?

He tucked the matter away in a corner of his mind
for the moment; the answer would come to him later
on. He had a wonderfully retentive mind. Everything which he saw or heard seemed to make its cor-
responding impression somewhere in his brain; often
without his being conscious of it; and these photo-
graphic impressions were always there ready for him
when he wished to develop them.

Cayley joined him at the window.

"I've telephoned," he said. "They're sending an
inspector or some one from Middleston, and the
local police and doctor from Stanton." He shrugged
his shoulders. "We're in for it now."

"How far away is Middleston?" It was the town for which Antony had taken a ticket that morning—only six hours ago. How absurd it seemed.

"About twenty miles. These people will be coming back soon."

"Beverley, and the others?"

"Yes. I expect they'll want to go away at once."

"Much better that they should."

"Yes." Cayley was silent for a little. Then he said, "You're staying near here?"

"I'm at the 'George,' at Woodham."

"If you're by yourself, I wish you'd put up here. You see," he went on awkwardly, "you'll have to *be* here—for the—inquest and—and so on. If I may offer you my cousin's hospitality in his—I mean if he doesn't —if he really has——"

Antony broke in hastily with his thanks and acceptance.

"That's good. Perhaps Beverley will stay on, if he's a friend of yours. He's a good fellow."

Antony felt quite sure, from what Cayley had said and had hesitated to say, that Mark had been the last to see his brother alive. It didn't follow that Mark Ablett was a murderer. Revolvers go off accidentally; and when they have gone off, people lose their heads and run away, fearing that their story will not be believed. Nevertheless, when people run away, whether innocently or guiltily, one can't help wondering which way they went.

"I suppose this way," said Antony aloud, looking out of the window.

"Who?" said Cayley stubbornly.

"Well, whoever it was," said Antony, smiling to himself. "The murderer. Or, let us say, the man who locked the door after Robert Ablett was killed."

"I wonder."

"Well, how else could he have got away? He didn't go by the windows in the next room, because they were shut."

"Isn't that rather odd?"

"Well, I thought so at first, but——" He pointed to the wall jutting out on the right. "You see, you're protected from the rest of the house if you get out here, and you're quite close to the shrubbery. If you go out at the French windows, I imagine you're much more visible. All that part of the house——" he waved his right hand—"the west, well, north-west almost, where the kitchen parts are—you see, you're hidden from them here. Oh, yes! he knew the house, whoever it was, and he was quite right to come out of this window. He'd be into the shrubbery at once."

Cayley looked at him thoughtfully.

"It seems to me, Mr. Gillingham, that *you* know the house pretty well, considering that this is the first time you've been to it."

Antony laughed.

"Oh, well, I notice things, you know. I was born noticing. But I'm right, aren't I, about why he went out this way?"

"Yes, I think you are." Cayley looked away—towards the shrubbery. "Do you want to go noticing in *there* now?" He nodded at it.

"I think we might leave that to the police," said Antony gently. "It's—well, there's no hurry."

Cayley gave a little sigh, as if he had been holding his breath for the answer and could now breathe again.

"Thank you, Mr. Gillingham," he said.

CHAPTER IV

THE BROTHER FROM AUSTRALIA

Guests at the Red House were allowed to do what they liked within reason—the reasonableness or otherwise of it being decided by Mark. But when once they (or Mark) had made up their minds as to what they wanted to do, the plan had to be kept. Mrs. Calladine, who knew this little weakness of their host's, resisted, therefore, the suggestion of Bill that they should have a second round in the afternoon, and drive home comfortably after tea. The other golfers were willing enough, but Mrs. Calladine, without actually saying that Mr. Ablett wouldn't like it, was firm on the point that, having arranged to be back by four, they should be back by four.

"I really don't think Mark wants us, you know," said the Major. Having played badly in the morning, he wanted to prove to himself in the afternoon that he was really better than that. "With this brother of his coming, he'll be only too glad to have us out of the way."

"Of course he will, Major." This from Bill. "You'd like to play, wouldn't you, Miss Norris?"

Miss Norris looked doubtfully at the hostess.

"Of course, if you want to get back, dear, we mustn't keep you here. Besides, it's so dull for you, not playing."

"Just nine holes, mother," pleaded Betty.

"The car could take you back, and you could tell them that we were having another round, and then it could come back for us," said Bill brilliantly.

"It's certainly much cooler here than I expected," put in the Major.

Mrs. Calladine fell. It was very pleasantly cool outside the golf-house, and of course Mark *would* be rather glad to have them out of the way. So she consented to nine holes; and the match having ended all-square, and everybody having played much better than in the morning, they drove back to the Red House, very well pleased with themselves.

"Hallo," said Bill to himself, as they approached the house, "isn't that old Tony?"

Antony was standing in front of the house, waiting for them. Bill waved, and he waved back. Then as the car drew up, Bill, who was in front with the chauffeur, jumped down and greeted him eagerly.

"Hallo, you madman, have you come to stay, or what?" He had a sudden idea. "*Don't* say you're Mark Ablett's long-lost brother from Australia, though I could quite believe it of you." He laughed boyishly.

"Hallo, Bill," said Antony quietly. "Will you introduce me? I'm afraid I've got some bad news."

Bill, rather sobered by this, introduced him. The Major and Mrs. Calladine were on the near side of the car, and Antony spoke to them in a low voice.

"I'm afraid I'm going to give you rather a shock," he said. "Robert Ablett, Mr. Mark Ablett's brother, has been killed." He jerked a thumb over his shoulder. "In the house."

"Good God!" said the Major.

"Do you mean that he has killed himself?" asked Mrs. Calladine. "Just now?"

"It was about two hours ago. I happened to come here"—he half-turned to Beverley and explained—"I was coming to see *you*, Bill, and I arrived just after the—the death. Mr. Cayley and I found the body. Mr. Cayley being busy just now—there are police and doctors and so on in the house—he asked me to tell you. He says that no doubt you would prefer, the house-party having been broken up in this tragic way, to leave as soon as possible." He gave a pleasant apologetic little smile and went on. "I am putting it badly, but what he means, of course, is that you must consult your own feelings in the matter entirely, and please make your own arrangements about ordering the car for whatever train you wish to catch. There is one this evening, I understand, which you could go by if you wished it."

Bill gazed with open mouth at Antony. He had no words in his vocabulary to express what he wanted to say, other than those the Major had already used. Betty was leaning across to Miss Norris and saying, "*Who's* killed?" in an awe-struck voice, and Miss Norris, who was instinctively looking as tragic as she looked on the stage when a messenger announced the deaths of one of the cast, stopped for a moment in order to explain. Mrs. Calladine was quietly mistress of herself.

"We shall be in the way, yes, I quite understand," she said; "but we can't just shake the dust of the place off our shoes because something terrible has happened there. I must see Mark, and we can arrange later what to do. He must know how very deeply we feel for him. Perhaps we——" she hesitated.

"The Major and I might be useful anyway," said Bill. "Isn't that what you mean, Mrs. Calladine?"

"Where *is* Mark?" said the Major suddenly, looking hard at Antony.

Antony looked back unwaveringly—and said nothing.

"I think," said the Major gently, leaning over to Mrs. Calladine, "that it would be better if you took Betty back to London to-night."

"Very well," she agreed quietly. "You will come with us, Ruth?"

"I'll see you safely there," said Bill in a meek voice. He didn't quite know what was happening, and, having expected to stay at the Red House for another week, he had nowhere to go to in London, but London seemed to be the place that everyone was going to, and when he could get Tony alone for a moment, Tony no doubt would explain.

"Cayley wants you to stay, Bill. You have to go anyhow, tomorrow, Major Rumbold?"

"Yes. I'll come with you, Mrs. Calladine."

"Mr. Cayley would wish me to say again that you will please not hesitate to give your own orders, both as regards the car and as regards any telephoning or telegraphing that you want done." He smiled again and added, "Please forgive me if I seem to have taken a good deal upon myself, but I just happened to be handy as a mouthpiece for Cayley." He bowed to them and went into the house.

"Well!" said Miss Norris dramatically.

As Antony re-entered the hall, the Inspector from Middleston was just crossing into the library with Cayley. The latter stopped and nodded to Antony.

"Wait a moment, Inspector. Here's Mr. Gilling-

ham. He'd better come with us." And then to Antony.
"This is Inspector Birch."

Birch looked inquiringly from one to the other.

"Mr. Gillingham and I found the body together,"
explained Cayley.

"Oh! Well, come along, and let's gets the facts
sorted out a bit. I like to know where I am, Mr.
Gillingham."

"We all do."

"Oh!" He looked at Antony with interest. "D'you
know where you are in this case?"

"I know where I'm going to be."

"Where's that?"

"Put through it by Inspector Birch," said Antony
with a smile.

The inspector laughed genially.

"Well, I'll spare you as much as I can. Come along."

They went into the library. The inspector seated
himself at a writing-table, and Cayley sat in a chair
by the side of it. Antony made himself comfortable
in an armchair and prepared to be interested.

"We'll start with the dead man," said the inspector.
"Robert Ablett, didn't you say?" He took out his
notebook.

"Yes. Brother of Mark Ablett, who lives here."

"Ah!" He began to sharpen a pencil. "Staying in
the house?"

"Oh, no!"

Antony listened attentively while Cayley explained
all that he knew about Robert. This was news to
him.

"I see. Sent out of the country in disgrace. What
had he done?"

"I hardly know. I was only about twelve at the

time. The sort of age when you're told not to ask questions."

"Inconvenient questions?"

"Exactly."

"So you don't really know whether he had been merely wild or—or wicked?"

"No. Old Mr. Ablett was a clergyman," added Cayley. "Perhaps what might seem wicked to a clergyman might seem only wild to a man of the world."

"I daresay, Mr. Cayley," smiled the inspector. "Anyhow, it was more convenient to have him in Australia?"

"Yes."

"Mark Ablett never talked about him?"

"Hardly ever. He was very much ashamed of him, and—well, very glad he was in Australia."

"Did he write Mark sometimes?"

"Occasionally. Perhaps three or four times in the last five years."

"Asking for money?"

"Something of the sort. I don't think Mark always answered them. As far as I know, he never sent any money."

"Now your own private opinion, Mr. Cayley. Do you think that Mark was unfair to his brother? Unduly hard on him?"

"They'd never liked each other as boys. There was never any affection between them. I don't know whose fault it was in the first place—if anybody's."

"Still, Mark might have given him a hand?"

"I understand," said Cayley, "that Robert spent his whole life asking for hands."

The inspector nodded.

"I know that sort. Well, now, we'll go on to this morning. This letter that Mark got—did you see it?"

"Not at the time. He showed it to me afterwards."

"Any address?"

"No. A half-sheet of rather dirty paper."

"Where is it now?"

"I don't know. In Mark's pocket, I expect."

"Ah!" He pulled at his beard. "Well, we'll come to that. Can you remember what it said?"

"As far as I remember, something like this: 'Mark, your loving brother is coming to see you to-morrow, all the way from Australia. I give you warning so that you will be able to conceal your surprise, but not I hope, your pleasure. Expect him at three, or thereabouts.'"

"Ah!" The inspector copied it down carefully. "Did you notice the postmark?"

"London."

"And what was Mark's attitude?"

"Annoyance, disgust——" Cayley hesitated.

"Apprehension?"

"N—no, not exactly. Or, rather, apprehension of an unpleasant interview, not of any unpleasant outcome for himself."

"You mean that he wasn't afraid of violence, or blackmail, or anything of that sort?"

"He didn't appear to be."

"Right. . . . Now then, he arrived, you say, about three o'clock?"

"Yes, about that."

"Who was in the house then?"

"Mark and myself, and some of the servants. I don't know which. Of course, you will ask them directly, no doubt."

"With your permission. No guests?"

"They were out all day playing golf," explained Cayley. "Oh, by the way," he put in, "if I may interrupt a moment, will you want to see them at all? It isn't very pleasant for them now, naturally, and I suggested——" he turned to Antony, who nodded back to him. "I understand that they want to go back to London this evening. There's no objection to that, I suppose?"

"You will let me have their names and addresses in case I want to communicate with them?"

"Of course. One of them is staying on, if you would like to see him later, but they only came back from their golf as we crossed the hall."

"That's all right, Mr. Cayley. Well, now then, let's go back to three o'clock. Where were you when Robert arrived?"

Cayley explained how he had been sitting in the hall, how Audrey had asked him where the master was, and how he had said that he had last seen him going up to the Temple.

"She went away, and I went on with my book. There was a step on the stairs, and I looked up to see Mark coming down. He went into the office, and I went on with my book again. I went into the library for a moment, to refer to another book, and when I was in there I heard a shot. At least, it was a loud bang, I wasn't sure if it was a shot. I stood and listened. Then I came slowly to the door and looked out. Then I went back again, hesitated a bit, you know, and finally decided to go across to the office, and make sure that it was all right. I turned the handle of the door and found it was locked. Then I got frightened, and I banged at the door, and shouted, and—well, that was when Mr. Gillingham arrived." He went on to explain how they had found the body.

The inspector looked at him with a smile.

"Yes, well, we shall have to go over some of that again, Mr. Cayley. Mr. Mark, now. You thought he was in the Temple. Could he have come in, and gone up to his room, without your seeing him?"

"There are back stairs. He wouldn't have used them in the ordinary way, of course. But I wasn't in the hall all the afternoon. He might easily have gone upstairs without my knowing anything about it."

"So that you weren't surprised when you saw him coming down?"

"Oh, not a bit."

"Well, did he say anything?"

"He said, 'Robert's here?' or something of the sort. I suppose he'd heard the bell, or the voices in the hall."

"Which way does his bedroom face? Could he have seen him coming down the drive?"

"He might have, yes."

"Well?"

"Well, then, I said, 'Yes,' and he gave a sort of shrug, and said, 'Don't go too far away, I might want you'; and then went in."

"What did you think he meant by that?"

"Well, he consults me a good deal, you know. I'm his sort of unofficial solicitor in a kind of way."

"This was a business meeting rather than a brotherly one?"

"Oh, yes. That's how he regarded it, I'm sure."

"Yes. How long was it before you heard the shot?"

"Very soon. Two minutes, perhaps."

The inspector finished his writing, and then regarded Cayley thoughtfully. Suddenly he said:

"What is your theory of Robert's death?"

Cayley shrugged his shoulders.

"You've probably seen more than I've seen," he answered. "It's your job. I can only speak as a layman—and Mark's friend."

"Well?"

"Then I should say that Robert came here meaning trouble, and bringing a revolver with him. He produced it almost at once, Mark tried to get it from him, there was a little struggle perhaps, and it went off. Mark lost his head, finding himself there with a revolver in his hand and a dead man at his feet. His one idea was to escape. He locked the door instinctively, and then, when he heard me hammering at it, went out of the window."

"Y—yes. Well, that sounds reasonable enough. What do you say, Mr. Gillingham?"

"I should hardly call it 'reasonable' to lose your head," said Antony, getting up from his chair and coming towards them.

"Well, you know what I mean. It explains things."

"Oh, yes. Any other explanation would make them much more complicated."

"*Have* you any other explanation?"

"Not I."

"Are there any points on which you would like to correct Mr. Cayley?—anything that he left out after you arrived here?"

"No, thanks. He described it all very accurately."

"Ah! Well now, about yourself. You're not staying in the house, I gather?"

Antony explained his previous movements.

"Yes. Did you hear the shot?"

Antony put his head on one side, as if listening.

"Yes. Just as I came in sight of the house. It didn't make any impression at the time, but I remember it now."

"Where were you then?"

"Coming up the drive. I was just in sight of the house."

"Nobody left the house by the front door after the shot?"

Antony closed his eyes and considered.

"Nobody," he said. "No."

"You're certain of that?"

"Absolutely," said Antony, as though rather surprised that he could be suspected of a mistake.

"Thank you. You're at the 'George,' if I want you?"

"Mr. Gillingham is staying here until after the inquest," explained Cayley.

"Good. Well now, about these servants?"

CHAPTER V

MR. GILLINGHAM CHOOSES A NEW PROFESSION

As Cayley went over to the bell, Antony got up and moved to the door.

"Well, you won't want me, I suppose, inspector," he said.

"No, thank you, Mr. Gillingham. You'll be about, of course?"

"Oh, yes."

The inspector hesitated.

"I think, Mr. Cayley, it would be better if I saw the servants alone. You know what they are; the more people about, the more they get alarmed. I expect I can get at the truth better by myself."

"Oh, quite so. In fact, I was going to ask you to excuse me. I feel rather responsible towards these guests of ours. Although Mr. Gillingham very kindly——" He smiled at Antony, who was waiting at the door, and left his sentence unfinished.

"Ah, that reminds me," said the inspector. "Didn't you say that one of your guests—Mr. Beverley, was it?—a friend of Mr. Gillingham's, was staying on?"

"Yes; would you like to see him?"

"Afterwards, if I may."

"I'll warn him. I shall be up in my room, if you want me. I have a room upstairs where I work—any of the servants will show you. Ah, Stevens, Inspector Birch would like to ask you a few questions."

"Yes, sir," said Audrey primly, but inwardly fluttering.

The housekeeper's room had heard something of the news by this time, and Audrey had had a busy time explaining to other members of the staff exactly what *he* had said, and what *she* had said. The details were not quite established yet, but this much at least was certain: that Mr. Mark's brother had shot himself and spirited Mr. Mark away, and that Audrey had seen at once that he was that sort of man when she opened the door to him. She had passed the remark to Mrs. Stevens. And Mrs. Stevens—if you remember, Audrey—had always said that people didn't go away to Australia except for very good reasons. Elsie agreed with both of them, but she had a contribution of her own to make. She had actually heard Mr. Mark in the office, threatening his brother.

"You mean Mr. Robert," said the second parlourmaid. She had been having a little nap in her room, but she had heard the bang. In fact, it had woken her up—just like something going off, it was.

"It was Mr. Mark's voice," said Elsie firmly.

"Pleading for mercy," said an eager-eyed kitchenmaid hopefully from the door, and was hurried out again by the others, wishing that she had not given her presence away. But it was hard to listen in silence when she knew so well from her novelettes just what happened on these occasions.

"I shall have to give that girl a piece of my mind," said Mrs. Stevens. "Well, Elsie?"

"He said, I heard him say it with my own ears, 'It's my turn now,' he said triumphant-like."

"Well, if you think that's a threat, dear, you're very particular, I must say."

But Audrey remembered Elsie's words when she was in front of Inspector Birch. She gave her own evidence with the readiness of one who had already repeated it several times, and was examined and cross-examined by the inspector with considerable skill. The temptation to say, "Never mind about what *you* said to *him*," was strong, but he resisted it, knowing that in this way he would discover best what *he* said to *her*. By this time both his words and the looks he gave her were getting their full value from Audrey, but the general meaning of them seemed to be well-established.

"Then you didn't see Mr. Mark at all?"

"No, sir; he must have come in before and gone up to his room. Or come in by the front door, likely enough, while I was going out by the back."

"Yes. Well, I think that's all that I want to know, thank you very much. Now what about the other servants?"

"Elsie heard the master and Mr. Robert talking together," said Audrey eagerly. "He was saying—Mr. Mark, I mean——"

"Ah! Well, I think Elsie had better tell me that herself. Who is Elsie, by the way?"

"One of the housemaids. Shall I send her to you, sir?"

"Please."

Elsie was not sorry to get the message. It interrupted a few remarks from Mrs. Stevens about Elsie's conduct that afternoon which were (Elsie thought) much better interrupted. In Mrs. Stevens' opinion any crime committed that afternoon in the office was as nothing to the double crime committed by the unhappy Elsie.

For Elsie realized too late that she would have done better to have said nothing about her presence in the hall that afternoon. She was bad at concealing the truth and Mrs. Stevens was good at discovering it. Elsie knew perfectly well that she had no business to come down the front stairs, and it was no excuse to say that she happened to come out of Miss Norris' room just at the head of the stairs, and didn't think it would matter, as there was nobody in the hall, and what was she doing anyhow in Miss Norris' room at that time? Returning a magazine? Lent by Miss Norris, might she ask? Well, not exactly lent. Really, Elsie!—and this in a respectable house! In vain for poor Elsie to plead that a story by her favourite author was advertised on the cover, with a picture of the villain falling over the cliff. "That's where *you'll* go to, my girl, if you aren't careful," said Mrs. Stevens firmly.

But, of course, there was no need to confess all these crimes to Inspector Birch. All that interested him was that she was passing through the hall, and heard voices in the office.

"And stopped to listen?"

"Certainly not," said Elsie with dignity, feeling that nobody really understood her. "I was just passing through the hall, just as you might have been yourself, and not supposing they were talking secrets, didn't think to stop my ears, as no doubt I ought to have done." And she sniffed slightly.

"Come, come," said the inspector soothingly, "I didn't mean to suggest——"

"Everyone is very unkind to me," said Elsie between sniffs, "and there's that poor man lying dead there, and sorry they'd have been, if it had been me, to have spoken to me as they have done this day."

"Nonsense, we're going to be very proud of you. I shouldn't be surprised if your evidence were of very great importance. Now then, what was it you heard? Try to remember the exact words."

Something about working in a passage, thought Elsie.

"Yes, but who said it?"

"Mr. Robert."

"How do you know it was Mr. Robert? Had you heard his voice before?"

"I don't take it upon myself to say that I had had any acquaintance with Mr. Robert, but seeing that it wasn't Mr. Mark, nor yet Mr. Cayley, nor any other of the gentlemen, and Miss Stevens had shown Mr. Robert into the office not five minutes before——"

"Quite so," said the inspector hurriedly. "Mr. Robert, undoubtedly. Working in a passage?"

"That was what it sounded like, sir."

"H'm. Working a passage over—could that have been it?"

"That's right, sir," said Elsie eagerly. "He'd worked his passage over."

"Well?"

"And then Mr. Mark said loudly—sort of triumphant-like—'It's *my* turn now. You wait.'"

"Triumphantly?"

"As much as to say his chance had come."

"And that's all you heard?"

"That's all, sir—not standing there listening, but just passing through the hall, as it might be any time."

"Yes. Well, that's really very important, Elsie. Thank you."

Elsie gave him a smile, and returned eagerly to the kitchen. She was ready for Mrs. Stevens or anybody now.

Meanwhile Antony had been exploring a little on his own. There was a point which was puzzling him. He went through the hall to the front of the house and stood at the open door, looking out on to the drive. He and Cayley had run round the house to the left. Surely it would have been quicker to have run round to the right? The front door was not in the middle of the house, it was to the end. Undoubtedly they went the longest way round. But perhaps there was something in the way, if one went to the right—a wall, say. He strolled off in that direction, followed a path round the house and came in sight of the office windows. Quite simple, and about half the distance of the other way. He went on a little farther, and came to a door, just beyond the broken-in windows. It opened easily, and he found himself in a passage. At the end of the passage was another door. He opened it and found himself in the hall again.

"And, of course, that's the quickest way of the three," he said to himself. "Through the hall, and out at the back; turn to the left and there you are. Instead of which, we ran the longest way round the house. Why? Was it to give Mark more time in which to escape? Only, in that case—why *run*? Also, how did Cayley know then that it was Mark who was trying to escape? If he had guessed—well, not guessed, but been afraid—that one had shot the other, it was much more likely that Robert had shot Mark. Indeed, he had admitted that this was what he thought. The first thing he had said when he turned the body over was, 'Thank God! I was afraid it was Mark.' But why should he want to give *Robert* time in which to get away? And again—why *run*, if he did want to give him time?"

Antony went out of the house again to the lawns at the back, and sat down on a bench in view of the office windows.

"Now then," he said, "let's go through Cayley's mind carefully, and see what we get."

Cayley had been in the hall when Robert was shown into the office. The servant goes off to look for Mark, and Cayley goes on with his book. Mark comes down the stairs, warns Cayley to stand by in case he is wanted, and goes to meet his brother. What does Cayley expect? Possibly that he won't be wanted at all; possibly that his advice may be wanted in the matter, say, of paying Robert's debts, or getting him a passage back to Australia; possibly that his physical assistance may be wanted to get an obstreperous Robert out of the house. Well, he sits there for a moment, and then goes into the library. Why not? He is still within reach, if wanted. Suddenly he hears a pistol-shot. A pistol-shot is the last noise you expect to hear in a countryhouse; very natural, then, that for the moment he would hardly realize what it was. He listens—and hears nothing more. Perhaps it wasn't a pistol-shot after all. After a moment or two he goes to the library door again. The profound silence makes him uneasy now. *Was* it a pistol-shot? Absurd! Still—no harm in going into the office on some excuse, just to reassure himself. So he tries the door—and finds it locked!

What are his emotions now? Alarm, uncertainty. Something is happening. Incredible though it seems, it must have been a pistol-shot. He is banging at the door and calling out to Mark, and there is no answer. Alarm—yes. But alarm for whose safety? Mark's, obviously. Robert is a stranger; Mark is an intimate friend. Robert has written a letter that morning, the letter of a man in a dangerous temper. Robert is the tough customer; Mark the highly civilized gentleman. If there has been a quarrel, it is Robert who has shot Mark. He bangs at the door again.

Of course, to Antony, coming suddenly upon this scene, Cayley's conduct had seemed rather absurd, but then, just for the moment, Cayley had lost his head. Anybody else might have done the same. But, as soon as Antony suggested trying the windows, Cayley saw that that was the obvious thing to do. So he leads the way to the windows—the longest way.

Why? To give the murderer time to escape? If he had thought then that Mark was the murderer, perhaps, yes. But he thinks that Robert is the murderer. If he is not hiding anything, he *must* think so. Indeed he says so, when he sees the body; "I was afraid it was Mark," he says, when he finds that it is Robert who is killed. No reason, then, for wishing to gain time. On the contrary, every instinct would urge him to get into the room as quickly as possible, and seize the wicked Robert. Yet he goes the longest way round. Why? And then, why *run?*

"That's the question," said Antony to himself, as he filled his pipe, "and bless me if I know the answer. It may be, of course, that Cayley is just a coward. He was in no hurry to get close to Robert's revolver, and yet wanted me to think that he was bursting with eagerness. That would explain it, but then that makes Cayley out a coward. Is he? At any rate he pushed his face up against the window bravely enough. No, I want a better answer than that."

He sat there with his unlit pipe in his hand thinking. There were one or two other things in the back
of his brain, waiting to be taken out and looked at.
For the moment he left them undisturbed. They
would come back to him later when he wanted them.

He laughed suddenly, and lit his pipe.

"I was wanting a new profession," he thought,
"and now I've found it. Antony Gillingham, our own
private sleuthhound. I shall begin to-day."

Whatever Antony Gillingham's other qualifications
for his new profession, he had at any rate a brain
which worked clearly and quickly. And this clear brain
of his had already told him that he was the only person
in the house at that moment who was unhandicapped
in the search for truth. The inspector had arrived
in it to find a man dead and a man missing. It was
extremely probable, no doubt, that the missing man
had shot the dead man. But it was more than extremely probable, it was almost certain that the inspector
would start with the idea that this extremely probable
solution was the one true solution, and that, in con-
sequence, he would be less disposed to consider without prejudice any other solution. As regards all the
rest of them—Cayley, the guests, the servants—they
also were prejudiced; in favour of Mark (or possibly,
for all he knew, against Mark); in favour of, or
against, each other; they had formed some previous
opinion, from what had been said that morning, of
the sort of man Robert was. No one of them could
consider the matter with an unbiased mind.

But Antony could. He knew nothing about Mark;
he knew nothing about Robert. He had seen the
dead man before he was told who the dead man was.

He knew that a tragedy had happened before he knew that anybody was missing. Those first impressions, which are so vitally important, had been received solely on the merits of the case; they were founded on the evidence of his senses, not on the evidence of his emotions or of other people's senses. He was in a much better position for getting at the truth than was the inspector.

It is possible that, in thinking this, Antony was doing Inspector Birch a slight injustice. Birch was certainly prepared to believe that Mark had shot his brother. Robert had been shown into the office (witness Audrey) ; Mark had gone in to Robert (witness Cayley) ; Mark and Robert had been heard talking (witness Elsie) ; there was a shot (witness everybody) ; the room had been entered and Robert's body had been found (witness Cayley and Gillingham). And Mark was missing. Obviously, then, Mark had killed his brother: accidentally, as Cayley believed, or deliberately, as Elsie's evidence seemed to suggest. There was no point in looking for a difficult solution to a problem, when the easy solution had no flaw in it. But at the same time Birch would have preferred the difficult solution, simply because there was more credit attached to it. A "sensational" arrest of somebody in the house would have given him more pleasure than a commonplace pursuit of Mark Ablett across country. Mark must be found, guilty or not guilty. But there were other possibilities. It would have interested Antony to know that, just at the time when he was feeling rather superior to the prejudiced inspector, the inspector himself was letting his mind dwell lovingly upon the possibilities in connexion with Mr. Gillingham. Was it only a coincidence that

Mr. Gillingham had turned up just when he did? And Mr. Beverley's curious answers when asked for some account of his friend. An assistant in a tobacconist's, a waiter! An odd man, Mr. Gillingham, evidently. It might be as well to keep an eye on him.

CHAPTER VI

OUTSIDE OR INSIDE?

The guests had said good-bye to Cayley, according to their different manner. The Major, gruff and simple: "If you want me, command me. Anything I can do—Goodbye"; Betty, silently sympathetic, with everything in her large eyes which she was too much over-awed to tell; Mrs. Calladine, protesting that she did not know *what* to say, but apparently finding plenty; and Miss Norris, crowding so much into one despairing gesture that Cayley's unvarying "Thank you very much" might have been taken this time as gratitude for an artistic entertainment.

Bill had seen them into the car, had taken his own farewells (with a special squeeze of the hand for Betty), and had wandered out to join Antony on his garden seat.

"Well, this is a rum show," said Bill as he sat down.

"Very rum, William."

"And you actually walked right into it?"

"Right into it," said Antony.

"Then you're the man I want. There are all sorts of rumours and mysteries about, and that inspector fellow simply wouldn't keep to the point when I wanted to ask him about the murder, or whatever it is, but kept asking me questions about where I'd met you first, and all sorts of dull things like that. Now what really happened?"

Antony told him as concisely as he could all that he had already told the inspector, Bill interrupting him here and there with appropriate "Good Lords" and whistles.

"I say, it's a bit of a business, isn't it? Where do *I* come in, exactly?"

"How do you mean?"

"Well, everybody else is bundled off except me, and I get put through it by that inspector as if I knew all about it—what's the idea?"

Antony smiled at him.

"Well, there's nothing to worry about, you know. Naturally Birch wanted to see one of you so as to know what you'd all been doing all day. And Cayley was nice enough to think that you'd be company for me, as I knew you already. And—well, that's all."

"You're staying here, in the house?" said Bill eagerly. "Good man. That's splendid."

"It reconciles you to the departure of—some of the others?"

Bill blushed.

"Oh, well, I shall see her again next week, anyway," he murmured.

"I congratulate you. I liked her looks. And that grey dress. A nice comfortable sort of woman——"

"You fool, that's her mother."

"Oh, I beg your pardon. But anyhow, Bill, I want you more than she does just now. So try and put up with me."

"I say, do you really?" asid Bill, rather flattered. He had a great admiration for Antony, and was very proud to be liked by him.

"Yes. You see, things are going to happen here soon."

"Inquests and that sort of thing?"

"Well, perhaps something before that. Hallo, here comes Cayley."

Cayley was walking across the lawn towards them, a big, heavy-shouldered man, with one of those strong, clean-shaven, ugly faces which can never quite be called plain.

"Bad luck on Cayley," said Bill. "I say, ought I to tell him how sorry I am and all that sort of thing? It seems so dashed inadequate."

"I shouldn't bother," said Antony.

Cayley nodded as he came to them, and stood there for a moment.

"We can make room for you," said Bill, getting up.

"Oh, don't bother, thanks. I just came to say," he went on to Antony, "that naturally they've rather lost their heads in the kitchen, and dinner won't be till half-past eight. Do just as you like about dressing, of course. And what about your luggage?"

"I thought Bill and I would walk over to the inn directly, and see about it."

"The car can go and fetch it as soon as it comes back from the station."

"It's very good of you, but I shall have to go over myself, anyhow, to pack up and pay my bill. Besides, it's a good evening for a walk. If you wouldn't mind it, Bill?"

"I should love it."

"Well, then, if you leave the bag there, I'll send the car round for it later."

"Thanks very much."

Having said what he wanted to say, Cayley remained there a little awkwardly, as if not sure whether to go or to stay. Antony wondered whether he wanted to talk about the afternoon's happenings, or whether it was the one subject he wished to avoid. To break the silence he asked carelessly if the inspector had gone.

Cayley nodded. Then he said abruptly, "He's getting a warrant for Mark's arrest."

Bill made a suitably sympathetic noise, and Antony said with a shrug of the shoulders, "Well, he was bound to do that, wasn't he? It doesn't follow that—well, it doesn't mean anything. They naturally want to get hold of your cousin, innocent or guilty."

"Which do you think he is, Mr. Gillingham?" said Cayley, looking at him steadily.

"Mark? It's absurd," said Bill impetuously.

"Bill's loyal, you see, Mr. Cayley."

"And you owe no loyalty to anyone concerned?"

"Exactly. So perhaps I might be too frank."

Bill had dropped down on the grass, and Cayley took his place on the seat, and sat there heavily, his elbows on his knees, his chin on his hands, gazing at the ground.

"I want you to be quite frank," he said at last. "Naturally I am prejudiced where Mark is concerned. So I want to know how my suggestion strikes you—who have no prejudices either way."

"Your suggestion?"

"My theory that, if Mark killed his brother, it was purely accidental—as I told the inspector."

Bill looked up with interest.

"You mean that Robert did the hold-up business," he said, "and there was a bit of a struggle, and the revolver went off, and then Mark lost his head and bolted? That sort of idea?"

"Exactly."

"Well, that seems all right." He turned to Antony. "There's nothing wrong with that, is there? It's the most natural explanation to anyone who knows Mark."

Antony pulled at his pipe.

"I suppose it is," he said slowly. "But there's one thing that worries me rather."

"What's that?" Bill and Cayley asked the question simultaneously.

"The key."

"The key?" said Bill.

Cayley lifted his head and looked at Antony. "What about the key?" he asked.

"Well there may be nothing in it; I just wondered. Suppose Robert was killed as you say, and suppose Mark lost his head and thought of nothing but getting away before anyone could see him. Well, very likely he'd lock the door and put the key in his pocket. He'd do it without thinking, just to gain a moment's time."

"Yes, that's what I suggest."

"It seems sound enough," said Bill. "Sort of thing you'd do without thinking, Besides, if you *are* going to run away, it gives you more of a chance."

"Yes, that's all right if the key is there. But suppose it isn't there?"

The suggestion, made as if it were already an established fact, startled them both. They looked at him wonderingly.

"What do you mean?" said Cayley.

"Well, it's just a question of where people happen

to keep their keys. You go up to your bedroom, and perhaps you like to lock your door in case anybody comes wandering in when you've only got one sock and a pair of braces on. Well, that's natural enough. And if you look around the bedrooms of almost any house, you'll find the keys all ready, so that you can lock yourself in at a moment's notice. But downstairs people don't lock themselves in. It's really never done at all. Bill, for instance, has never locked himself into the dining-room in order to be alone with the sherry. On the other hand, all women, and particularly servants, have a horror of burglars. And if a burglar gets in by the window, they like to limit his activities to that particular room. So they keep the keys on the *out*side of the doors, and lock the doors when they go to bed." He knocked the ashes out of his pipe, and added, "At least, my mother always used to."

"You mean," said Billy excitedly, "That the key was on the outside of the door when Mark went into the room?"

"Well, I was just wondering."

"Have you noticed the other rooms—the billiard-room, and library, and so on?" said Cayley.

"I've only just thought about it while I've been sitting out here. You live here—haven't *you* ever noticed them?"

Cayley sat considering, with his head on one side. "It seems rather absurd, you know, but I can't say that I have." He turned to Bill. "Have you?"

"Good Lord, no. I should never worry about a thing like that."

"I'm sure you wouldn't," laughed Antony. "Well, we can have a look when we go in. If the other keys are outside, then this one was probably outside too, and in that case—well, it makes it more interesting."

Cayley said nothing. Bill chewed a piece of grass thoughtfully, and then said, "Does it make much difference?"

"It makes it more hard to understand what happened in there. Take your accidental theory and see where you get to. No instinctive turning of the key now, is there? He's got to open the door to get it, and opening the door means showing his head to anybody in the hall—his cousin, for instance, whom he left there two minutes ago. Is a man in Mark's state of mind, frightened to death lest he should be found with the body, going to do anything so foolhardy as that?"

"He needn't have been afraid of *me,*" said Cayley.

"Then why didn't he call for you? He knew you were about. You could have advised him; Heaven knows he wanted advice. But the whole theory of Mark's escape is that he was afraid of you and of everybody else, and that he had no other idea but to get out of the room himself, and prevent you or the servants from coming into it. If the key had been on the inside, he would probably have locked the door. If it were on the outside, he almost certainly wouldn't."

"Yes, I expect you're right," said Bill thoughtfully. "Unless he took the key in with him, and locked the door at once."

"Exactly. But in that case you have to build up a new theory entirely."

"You mean that it makes it seem more deliberate?"

"Yes; that, certainly. But it also seems to make Mark out an absolute idiot. Just suppose for a moment that, for urgent reasons which neither of you know anything about, he had wished to get rid of his brother. Would he have done it like that? Just killed him and then run away? Why, that's practically suicide—suicide whilst of unsound mind. No. If you really wanted to remove an undesirable brother, you would do it a little bit more cleverly than that. You'd begin by treating him as a friend, so as to avoid suspicion, and when you did kill him at last, you would try to make it look like an accident, or suicide, or the work of some other man. Wouldn't you?"

"You mean you'd give yourself a bit of a run for your money?"

"Yes, that's what I mean. If you were going to do it deliberately, that is to say—and lock yourself in before you began."

Cayley had been silent, apparently thinking over this new idea. With his eyes still on the ground, he said now:

"I hold to my opinion that it was purely accidental, and that Mark lost his head and ran away."

"But what about the key?" asked Bill.

"We don't know yet that the keys *were* outside. I don't at all agree with Mr. Gillingham that the keys of the downstairs rooms are always outside the doors. Sometimes they are, no doubt; but I think we shall probably find that these are inside."

"Oh, well, of course, if they are inside, then your original theory is probably the correct one. Having often seen them outside, I just wondered—that's all. You asked me to be quite frank, you know, and tell you what I thought. But no doubt you're right, and we shall find them inside, as you say."

"Even if the key was outside," went on Cayley stubbornly, "I still think it might have been accidental. He might have taken it in with him, knowing that the interview would be an unpleasant one, and not wishing to be interrupted."

"But he had just told you to stand by in case he wanted you; so why should he lock you out? Besides, I should think that if a man were going to have an unpleasant interview with a threatening relation, the last thing he would do would be to barricade himself in with him. He would want to open all the doors and say, 'Get out of it!' "

Cayley was silent, but his mouth looked obstinate. Antony gave a little apologetic laugh and stood up.

"Well, come on, Bill," he said; "we ought to be stepping." He held out a hand and pulled his friend up. Then, turning to Cayley, he went on, "You must forgive me if I have let my thoughts run on rather. Of course, I was considering the matter purely as an outsider; just as a problem, I mean, which didn't concern the happiness of any of my friends."

"That's all right, Mr. Gillingham," said Cayley, standing up too. "It is for you to make allowances for *me*. I'm sure you will. You say that you're going up to the inn now about your bag?"

"Yes." He looked up at the sun and then round the parkland stretching about the house. "Let me see; it's over in *that* direction, isn't it?" He pointed southwards. "Can we get to the village that way, or must we go by the road?"

"I'll show you, my boy," said Bill.

"Bill will show you. The park reaches almost as far as the village. Then I'll send the car round in about half an hour."

"Thanks very much."

Cayley nodded and turned to go into the house. Antony took hold of Bill's arm and walked off with him in the opposite direction.

CHAPTER VII

PORTRAIT OF A GENTLEMAN

They walked in silence for a little, until they had left the house and gardens well behind them. In front of them and to the right the park dipped and then rose slowly, shutting out the rest of the world. A thick belt of trees on the left divided them from the main road.

"Ever been here before?" said Antony suddenly.

"Oh, rather. Dozens of times."

"I meant just here—where we are now. Or do you stay indoors and play billiards all the time?"

"Oh lord, no!"

"Well, tennis and things. So many people with beautiful parks never by any chance use them, and all the poor devils passing by on the dusty road think how lucky the owners are to have them, and imagine them doing all sorts of jolly things inside." He pointed to the right. "Ever been over there?"

Bill laughed, as if a little ashamed.

"Well, not very much. I've often been along here, of course, because it's the short way to the village."

"Yes. . . . All right; now tell me something about Mark."

"What sort of things?"

"Well, never mind about his being your host, or about your being a perfect gentleman, or anything

like that. Cut out the Manners for Men, and tell
me what you think of Mark, and how you like staying with him, and how many rows your little house-
party has had this week, and how you get on with
Cayley, and all the rest of it."

Bill looked at him eagerly.

"I say, are you being the complete detective?"

"Well, I wanted a new profession," smiled the other.

"What fun! I mean," he corrected himself apologetically, "one oughtn't to say that, when there's a
man dead in the house, and one's host——" He
broke off a little uncertainly, and then rounded off
his period by saying again, "By Jove, what a rum
show it is. Good Lord!"

"Well?" said Antony. "Carry on. Mark."

"What do I think of him?"

"Yes."

Bill was silent, wondering how to put into words
thoughts which had never formed themselves very
definitely in his own mind. What *did* he think of
Mark? Seeing his hesitation, Antony said:

"I ought to have warned you that nothing that you
say will be taken down by the reporters, so you
needn't bother about a split infinitive or two. Talk
about anything you like, how you like. Well, I'll
give you a start. Which do you enjoy more—a week-
end here or at the Barringtons, say?"

"Well, of course, that would depend——"

"Take it that she was there in both cases."

"Ass," said Bill, putting an elbow into Antony's
ribs. "It's a little difficult to say," he went on. "Of
course they do you awfully well here."

"Yes?"

"Yes. I don't think I know any house where things

are so comfortable. One's room—the food—drinks—cigars—the way everything's arranged. All that sort of thing. They look after you awfully well."

"Yes?"

"Yes." He repeated it slowly to himself, as if it had given him a new idea: "They look after you awfully well. Well, that's just what it is about Mark. That's one of his little ways. Weaknesses. Looking after you."

"Arranging things for you?"

"Yes. Of course, it's a delightful house, and there's plenty to do, and opportunities for every game or sport that's ever been invented, and, as I say, one gets awfully well done; but with it all, Tony, there's a faint sort of feeling that—well, that one is on parade, as it were. You've got to do as you're told."

"How do you mean?"

"Well, Mark fancies himself rather at arranging things. He arranges things, and it's understood that the guests fall in with the arrangement. For instance, Betty—Miss Calladine—and I were going to play a single just before tea, the other day. Tennis. She's frightfully hot stuff at tennis, and backed herself to take me on level. I'm rather erratic, you know. Mark saw us going out with our rackets and asked us what we were going to do. Well, he'd got up a little tournament for us after tea—handicaps all arranged by him, and everything ruled out neatly in red and black ink—prizes and all—quite decent ones, you know. He'd had the lawn specially cut and marked for it. Well, of course Betty and I wouldn't have spoilt the court, and we'd have been quite ready to play again after tea—I had to give her half-fifteen according to his handicap—but somehow——" Bill stopped and shrugged his shoulders.

"It didn't quite fit in?"

"No. It spoilt the effect of his tournament. Took the edge off it just a little, I suppose he felt. So we didn't play." He laughed, and added, "It would have been as much as our place was worth to have played."

"Do you mean you wouldn't have been asked here again?"

"Probably. Well, I don't know. Not for some time, anyway."

"Really, Bill?"

"Oh, rather! He's a devil for taking offence. That Miss Norris—did you see her—*she's* done for herself. I don't mind betting what you like that *she* never comes here again."

"Why?"

Bill laughed to himself.

"We were all in it, really—at least, Betty and I were. There's supposed to be a ghost attached to the house. Lady Anne Patten. Ever heard of her?"

"Never."

"Mark told us about her at dinner one night. He rather liked the idea of there being a ghost in his house, you know; except that he doesn't believe in ghosts. I think he wanted all of *us* to believe in her, and yet he was annoyed with Betty and Mrs. Calladine for believing in ghosts at all. Rum chap. Well, anyhow, Miss Norris—she's an actress, some actress too—dressed up as the ghost and played the fool a bit. Just for a moment, you know."

"What about the others?"

"Well, Betty and I knew; in fact, I'd told her— Miss Norris I mean—not to be a silly ass. Knowing Mark. Mrs. Calladine wasn't there—Betty wouldn't let her be. As for the Major, I don't believe anything would frighten *him*."

"Where did the ghost appear?"

"Down by the bowling-green. That's supposed to be its haunt, you know. We were all down there in the moonlight, pretending to wait for it. Do you know the bowling-green?"

"No."

"I'll show it to you after dinner."

"I wish you would. . . . Was Mark very angry afterwards?"

"Oh, Lord, yes. Sulked for a whole day. Well, he's just like that."

"Was he angry with all of you?"

"Oh, yes—sulky, you know."

"This morning?"

"Oh, no. He got over it—he generally does. He's just like a child. That's really it, Tony; he's like a child in some ways. As a matter of fact, he was unusually bucked with himself this morning. And yesterday."

"Yesterday?"

"Rather. We all said we'd never seen him in such form."

"Is he generally in form?"

"He's quite good company, you know, if you take him the right way. He's rather vain and childish—well, like I've been telling you—and self-important; but quite amusing in his way, and——" Bill broke off suddenly. "I say, you know, it really is the limit, talking about your host like this."

"Don't think of him as your host. Think of him as a suspected murderer with a warrant out against him."

"Oh! but that's all rot, you know."

"It's the fact, Bill."

"Yes, but I mean, he didn't do it. He wouldn't murder anybody. It's a funny thing to say, but—well, he's not big enough for it. He's got his faults, like all of us, but they aren't on that scale."

"One can kill anybody in a childish fit of temper."

Bill grunted assent, but without prejudice to Mark. "All the same," he said, "I can't believe it. That he would do it deliberately, I mean."

"Suppose it was an accident, as Cayley says, would he lose his head and run away?"

Bill considered for a moment.

"Yes, I really think he might, you know. He nearly ran away when he saw the ghost. Of course, that's different, rather."

"Oh, I don't know. In each case it's a question of obeying your instinct instead of your reason."

They had left the open land and were following a path through the bordering trees. Two abreast was uncomfortable, so Antony dropped behind, and further conversation was postponed until they were outside the boundary fence and in the high road. The road sloped gently down to the village of Woodham—a few red-roofed cottages, and the grey tower of a church showing above the green.

"Well, now," said Antony, as they stepped out more quickly, "what about Cayley?"

"How do you mean, what about him?"

"I want to see him. I can see Mark perfectly, thanks to you, Bill. You were wonderful. Now let's have Cayley's character. Cayley from within."

Bill laughed in pleased embarrassment, and protested that he was not a blooming novelist.

"Besides," he added, "Mark's easy. Cayley's one of these heavy, quiet people, who might be thinking about anything. Mark gives himself away. . . . Ugly, black-jawed devil, isn't he?"

"Some women like that type of ugliness."

"Yes, that's true. Between ourselves, I think there's one here who does. Rather a pretty girl at Jallands"—he waved his left hand—"down that way."

"What's Jallands?"

"Well, I suppose it used to be a farm, belonging to a bloke called Jalland, but now it's a country cottage belonging to a widow called Norbury. Mark and Cayley used to go there a good deal together. Miss Norbury—the girl—has been here once or twice for tennis; seemed to prefer Cayley to the rest of us. But of course he hadn't much time for that sort of thing."

"What sort of thing?"

"Walking about with a pretty girl and asking her if she's been to any theatres lately. He nearly always had something to do."

"Mark kept him busy?"

"Yes. Mark never seemed quite happy unless he had Cayley doing something for him. He was quite lost and helpless without him. And, funnily enough, Cayley seemed lost without Mark."

"He was fond of him?"

"Yes, I should say so. In a protective kind of way. He'd sized Mark up, of course—his vanity, his self-importance, his amateurishness and all the rest of it—but he liked looking after him. And he knew how to manage him."

"Yes. . . . What sort of terms was he on with the guests—you and Miss Norris and all of them?"

"Just polite and rather silent, you know. Keeping himself to himself. We didn't see so very much of him, except at meals. We were here to enjoy ourselves, and—well, *he* wasn't."

"He wasn't there when the ghost walked?"

"No. I heard Mark calling for him when he went

back to the house. I expect Cayley stroked down his feathers a bit, and told him that girls will be girls. . . . Hallo, here we are."

They went into the inn, and while Bill made himself pleasant to the landlady, Antony went upstairs to his room. It appeared that he had not very much packing to do, after all. He returned his brushes to his bag, glanced round to see that nothing else had been taken out, and went down again to settle his bill. He had decided to keep on his room for a few days; partly to save the landlord and his wife the disappointment of losing a guest so suddenly, partly in case he found it undesirable later on to remain at the Red House. For he was taking himself seriously (while getting all the fun out of it which was possible) at every new profession he adopted; and he felt that there might come a time—after the inquest, say—when he could not decently remain at the Red House as a guest, a friend of Bill's enjoying the hospitality of Mark or Cayley, whichever was to be regarded as his host, without forfeiting his independent attitude towards the events of that afternoon. At present he was staying in the house merely as a necessary witness, and, since he was there, Cayley could not object to him using his eyes; but if, after the inquest, it appeared that there was still work for a pair of independent and very keen eyes to do, then he must investigate, either with his host's approval or from beneath the roof of some other host; the landlord of the "George," for instance, who had no feelings in the matter.

For of one thing Antony was certain. Cayley knew more than he professed to know. That is to say, he knew more than he wanted other people to know he knew. Antony was one of the "other people"; if, therefore, he was for trying to find out what it was that Cayley knew, he could hardly expect Cayley's approval of his labours. It would be the "George," then, for Antony after the inquest.

What was the truth? Not necessarily discreditable to Cayley, even though he were hiding something. All that could be said against him at the moment was that he had gone the longest way round to get into the locked office—and that this did not fit in with what he had told the inspector. But it did fit in with the theory that he had been an accessory after the event, and that he wanted (while appearing to be in a hurry) to give his cousin as much time as possible in which to escape. That might not be the true solution, but it was at least a workable one. The theory which he had suggested to the inspector was not.

However, there would be a day or two before the inquest, in which Antony could consider all these matters from within the Red House. The car was at the door. He got in with Bill, the landlord put his bag on the front seat next to the chauffeur, and they drove back.

CHAPTER VIII

"DO YOU FOLLOW ME, WATSON?"

Antony's bedroom looked over the park at the back of the house. The blinds were not yet drawn while he was changing his clothes for dinner, and at various stages of undress he would pause and gaze out of the window, sometimes smiling to himself, sometimes frowning, as he turned over in his mind all the strange things that he had seen that day. He was sitting on his bed, in shirt and trousers absently smoothing down his thick black hair with his brushes, when Bill shouted an "Hallo!" through the door, and came in.

"I say, buck up, old boy, I'm hungry," he said cheerfully.

Antony stopped smoothing himself and looked up at him thoughtfully.

"Where's Mark?" he said.

"Mark? You mean Cayley."

Antony corrected himself with a little laugh. "Yes, I mean Cayley. Is he down? I say, I shan't be a moment, Bill." He got up from the bed and went on briskly with his dressing.

"Oh, by the way," said Bill, taking his place on the bed, "your idea about the keys is a wash-out."

"Why, how do you mean?"

"I went down just now and had a look at them. We were asses not to have thought of it when we came in. The library key is outside, but all the others are inside."

"Yes, I know."

"You devil, I suppose you did think of it, then?"

"I did, Bill," said Antony apologetically.

"Bother! I hoped you'd forgotten. Well, that knocks your theory on the head, doesn't it?"

"I never had a theory. I only said that *if* they were outside, it would probably mean that the office key was outside, and that in that case Cayley's theory was knocked on the head."

"Well, now, it isn't, and we don't know anything. Some were outside and some inside, and there you are. It makes it much less exciting. When you were talking about it on the lawn, I really got quite keen on the idea of the key being outside and Mark taking it in with him."

"It's going to be exciting enough," said Antony mildly, as he transferred his pipe and tobacco into the pocket of his black coat. "Well, let's come down; I'm ready now."

Cayley was waiting for them in the hall. He made some polite inquiry as to the guest's comfort, and the three of them fell into a casual conversation about houses in general and the Red House in particular.

"You were quite right about the keys," said Bill, during a pause. He was less able than the other two, perhaps because he was younger than they, to keep away from the subject which was uppermost in the minds of them all.

"Keys?" said Cayley blankly.

"We were wondering whether they were outside or inside."

"Oh! oh, yes!" He looked slowly round the hall, at the different doors, and then smiled in a friendly way at Antony. "We both seem to have been right, Mr. Gillingham. So we don't get much farther."

"No." He gave a shrug. "I just wondered, you know. I thought it was worth mentioning."

"Oh, quite. Not that you would have convinced me, you know. Just as Elsie's evidence doesn't convince me."

"Elsie?" said Bill excitedly. Antony looked inquiringly at him, wondering who Elsie was.

"One of the housemaids," explained Cayley. "You didn't hear what she told the inspector? Of course, as I told Birch, girls of that class make things up, but he seemed to think she was genuine."

"What was it?" said Bill.

Cayley told them of what Elsie had heard through the office door that afternoon.

"You were in the library then, of course," said Antony, rather to himself than to the other. "She might have gone through the hall without your hearing."

"Oh, I've no doubt she was there, and heard voices. Perhaps heard those very words. But——" He broke off, and then added impatiently, "It was accidental. I know it was accidental. What's the good of talking as if Mark was a murderer?" Dinner was announced at that moment, and as they went in, he added, "What's the good of talking about it at all, if it comes to that?"

"What, indeed?" said Antony, and to Bill's great disappointment they talked of books and politics during the meal.

Cayley made an excuse for leaving them as soon as their cigars were alight. He had business to attend to, as was natural. Bill would look after his friend. Bill was only too willing. He offered to beat Antony at billiards, to play him at piquet, to show him the garden by moonlight, or indeed to do anything else with him that he required.

"Thank the Lord you're here," he said piously. "I couldn't have stood it alone."

"Let's go outside," suggested Antony. "It's quite warm. Somewhere where we can sit down, right away from the house. I want to talk to you."

"Good man. What about the bowling-green?"

"Oh, you were going to show me that, anyhow, weren't you? Is it somewhere where we can talk without being overheard?"

"Rather. The ideal place. You'll see."

They came out of the front door and followed the drive to the left. Coming from Woodham, Antony had approached the house that afternoon from the other side. The way they were going now would take them out at the opposite end of the park, on the high road to Stanton, a country town some three miles away. They passed by a gate and a gardener's lodge, which marked the limit of what auctioneers like to call "the ornamental grounds of the estate," and then the open park was before them.

"Sure we haven't missed it?" said Antony. The park lay quietly in the moonlight on either side of the drive, wearing a little way ahead of them a deceptive air of smoothness which retreated always as they advanced.

"Rum, isn't it?" said Bill. "An absurd place for a bowling-green, but I suppose it was always here."

"Yes, but always where? It's short enough for golf, perhaps, but—Hallo!"

They had come to the place. The road bent round to the right, but they kept straight on over a broad

grass path for twenty yards, and there in front of
them was the green. A dry ditch, ten feet wide and six
feet deep, surrounded it, except in the one place where
the path went forward. Two or three grass steps led
down to the green, on which there was a long wooden
bench for the benefit of spectators.

"Yes, it hides itself very nicely," said Antony.
"Where do you keep the bowls?"

"In a sort of summer-house place. Round here."

They walked along the edge of the green until they
came to it—a low wooden bunk which had been built
into one wall of the ditch.

"H'm. Jolly view."

Bill laughed.

"Nobody sits there. It's just for keeping things out
of the rain."

They finished their circuit of the green—"Just in
case anybody's in the ditch," said Antony—and then
sat down on the bench.

"Now then," said Bill, "We are alone. Fire ahead."

Antony smoked thoughtfully for a little. Then he
took his pipe out of his mouth and turned to his
friend.

"Are you prepared to be the complete Watson?"
he asked.

"Watson?"

"Do-you-follow-me-Watson; that one. Are you prepared to have quite obvious things explained to you,
to ask futile questions, to give me chances of scor-
ing off you, to make brilliant discoveries of your
own two or three days after I have made them myself—all that kind of thing? Because it all helps."

"My dear Tony," said Bill delightedly, "need you
ask?" Antony said nothing, and Bill went on happily

to himself, "I perceive from the strawberry-mark on
your shirt-front that you had strawberries for dessert.
Holmes, you astonish me. Tut, tut, you know my
methods. Where is the tobacco? The tobacco is in the
Persian slipper. Can I leave my practice for a week?
I can."

Antony smiled and went on smoking. After waiting hopefully for a minute or two, Bill said in a firm
voice:

"Well then, Holmes, I feel bound to ask you if
you have deduced anything. Also whom do you
suspect?"

Antony began to talk.

"Do you remember," he said, "one of Holmes's
little scores over Watson about the number of steps
up to the Baker Street lodging? Poor old Watson
had been up and down them a thousand times, but
he had never thought of counting them, whereas
Holmes had counted them as a matter of course, and
knew that there were seventeen. And that was supposed to be the difference between the observation
and non-observation. Watson was crushed again, and
Holmes appeared to him more amazing than ever.
Now, it always seemed to me that in that matter
Holmes was the ass, and Watson the sensible person.
What on earth is the point of keeping in your head
an unnecessary fact like that? If you really want to
know at any time the number of steps to your lodging,
you can ring up your landlady and ask her. I've been
up and down the steps of the club a thousand times,
but if you asked me to tell you at this moment how
many steps there are I couldn't do it. Could you?"

"I certainly couldn't," said Bill.

"But if you really wanted to know," said Antony
casually, with a sudden change of voice, "I could

find out for you without even bothering to ring up the hall-porter."

Bill was puzzled as to why they were talking about the club steps, but he felt it his duty to say that he did want to know how many they were.

"Right," said Antony. "I'll find out."

He closed his eyes.

"I'm walking up St. James's Street," he said slowly. "Now I've come to the club and I'm going past the smoking-room windows—one—two—three—four. Now I'm at the steps. I turn in and begin going up them. One—two—three—four—five—six, then a broad step; six—seven—eight—nine, another broad step; nine—ten—eleven. Eleven—I'm inside. Good morning, Rogers. Fine day again." With a little start he opened his eyes and came back again to his present surroundings. He turned to Bill with a smile. "Eleven," he said. "Count them the next time you're there. Eleven—and now I hope I shall forget it again."

Bill was distinctly interested.

"That's rather hot," he said. "Expound."

"Well, I can't explain it, whether it's something in the actual eye, or something in the brain, or what, but I have got rather an uncanny habit of recording things unconsciously. You know that game where you look at a tray full of small objects for three minutes, and then turn away and try to make a list of them. It means a devil of a lot of concentration for the ordinary person, if he wants to get his list complete, but in some odd way I manage to do it without concentration at all. I mean that my eyes seem to do it without the brain consciously taking any part. I could look at the tray, for instance, and talk to you about golf at the same time, and still get my list right."

"I should think that's rather a useful gift for an amateur detective. You ought to have gone into the profession before."

"Well, it *is* rather useful. It's rather surprising, you know, to a stranger. Let's surprise Cayley with it, shall we?"

"How?"

"Well, let's ask him——" Antony stopped and looked at Bill comically—"let's ask him what he's going to do with the key to the office."

For a moment Bill did not understand.

"Key of the office?" he said vaguely. "You don't mean—Tony! What do you mean? Good God! do you mean that Cayley—But what about Mark?"

"I don't know where Mark is—that's another thing I want to know—but I'm quite certain that he hasn't got the key of the office with him. Because Cayley's got it."

"Are you sure?"

"Quite."

Bill looked at him wonderingly.

"I say," he said, almost pleadingly, "don't tell me that you can see into people's pockets and all that sort of thing—as well."

Antony laughed and denied it cheerfully.

"Then how do you know?"

"You're the perfect Watson, Bill. You take to it quite naturally. Properly speaking, I oughtn't to explain till the last chapter, but I always think that that's so unfair. So here goes. Of course, I don't really know that he's got it, but I do know that he had it. I know that when I came on him this afternoon, he had just locked the door and put the key in his pocket."

"You mean you saw him at the time, but that you've

only just remembered it—reconstructed it—in the way you were explaining just now?"

"No. I didn't see him. But I did see something. I saw the key of the billiard-room."

"Where?"

"Outside the billiard-room door."

"*Out*side? But it was inside when we looked just now."

"Exactly."

"Who put it there?"

"Obviously Cayley."

"But——"

"Let's go back to this afternoon. I don't remember noticing the billiard-room key at the time; I must have done so without knowing. Probably when I saw Cayley banging at the door I may have wondered subconsciously whether the key of the room next to it would fit. Something like that, I daresay. Well, when I was sitting out by myself on that seat just before you came along, I went over the whole scene in my mind, and I suddenly saw the billiard-room key there —outside. And I began to wonder if the office-key had been outside too. When Cayley came up, I told you my idea and you were both interested. But Cayley was just a shade too interested. I daresay you didn't notice it, but he was."

"By Jove!"

"Well, of course that proved nothing; and the key business didn't really prove anything, because whatever side of the door the other keys were, Mark might have locked his own private room from the inside sometimes. But I piled it on, and pretended that it was enormously important, and quite altered the case altogether, and having got Cayley thoroughly anxious about it, I told him that we should be well out of the

way for the next hour or so, and that he would be
alone in the house to do what he liked about it. And,
as I expected, he couldn't resist. He altered the keys
and gave himself away entirely."

"But the library key was still outside. Why didn't
he alter that?"

"Because he's a clever devil. For one thing, the inspector had been in the library, and might possibly
have noticed it already. And for another——" Antony
hesitated.

"What?" said Bill, after waiting for him to go on.

"It's only guesswork. But I fancy that Cayley was
thoroughly upset about the key business. He suddenly realized that he had been careless, and he
hadn't got time to think it all over. So he didn't want
to commit himself definitely to the statement that the
key was either outside or inside. He wanted to leave
it vague. It was safest that way."

"I see," said Bill slowly.

But his mind was elsewhere. He was wondering suddenly about Cayley. Cayley was just an ordinary man
—like himself. Bill had had little jokes with him sometimes; not that Cayley was much of a hand at jok-
ing. Bill had helped him to sausages, played tennis
with him, borrowed his tobacco, lent him a putter.
. . . and here was Antony saying that he was—what?
Well, not an ordinary man, anyway. A man with a
secret. Perhaps a—a murderer. No, not a murderer;
not Cayley. That was rot, anyway. Why, they had
played tennis together.

"Now then, Watson," said Antony suddenly. "It's
time you said something."

"I say, Tony, do you really mean it?"

"Mean what?"

"About Cayley."

"I mean what I said, Bill. No more."

"Well, what does it amount to?"

"Simply that Robert Ablett died in the office this afternoon, and that Cayley knows exactly how he died. That's all. It doesn't follow that Cayley killed him."

"No. No, of course it doesn't." Bill gave a sigh of relief. "He's just shielding Mark, what?"

"I wonder."

"Well, isn't that the simplest explanation?"

"It's the simplest if you're a friend of Cayley and want to let him down lightly. But then I'm not, you see."

"Why isn't it simple, anyhow?"

"Well, let's have the explanation then, and I'll undertake to give you a simpler one afterwards. Go on. Only remember—the key is on the outside of the door to start with."

"Yes; well, I don't mind that. Mark goes in to see his brother, and they quarrel and all the rest of it, just as Cayley was saying. Cayley hears the shot, and in order to give Mark time to get away, locks the door, puts the key in his pocket and pretends that Mark has locked the door, and that he can't get in. How's that?"

"Hopeless, Watson, hopeless."

"Why?"

"How does Cayley know that it is Mark who has shot Robert, and not the other way round?"

"Oh!" said Bill, rather upset. "Yes." He thought for a moment. "All right. Say that Cayley has gone into the room first, and seen Robert on the ground."

"Well?"

"Well, there you are."

"And what does he say to Mark? That it's a fine

afternoon, and could he lend him a pocket-handker-chief? Or does he ask him what's happened?"

"Well, of course, I suppose he asks what happened," said Bill reluctantly.

"And what does Mark say?"

"Explains that the revolver went off accidentally during a struggle."

"Whereupon Cayley shields him by—by doing what, Bill? Encouraging him to do the damn silliest thing that any man could possibly do—confess his guilt by running away!"

"No, that's rather hopeless, isn't it?" Bill thought again. "Well," he said reluctantly, "suppose Mark confessed that he'd murdered his brother?"

"That's better, Bill. Don't be afraid of getting away from the accident idea. Well then, your new theory is this. Mark confesses to Cayley that he shot Robert on purpose, and Cayley decides, even at the risk of committing perjury, and getting into the trouble himself, to help Mark to escape. Is that right?"

Bill nodded.

"Well then, I want to ask you two questions. First, is it possible, as I said before dinner, that any man would commit such an idiotic murder—a murder that puts the rope so very tightly round his neck? Secondly, if Cayley is prepared to perjure himself for Mark (as he has to, anyway, now), wouldn't it be simpler for him to say that he was in the office all the time, and that Robert's death was accidental?"

Bill considered this carefully, and then nodded slowly again.

"Yes, my simple explanation is a wash-out," he said. "Now let's have yours."

Antony did not answer him. He had begun to think about something quite different.

CHAPTER IX

POSSIBILITIES OF A CROQUET SET

"What's the matter?" said Bill sharply.

Antony looked round at him with raised eyebrows.

"You've thought of something suddenly," said Bill. "What is it?"

Antony laughed.

"My dear Watson," he said, "you aren't supposed to be as clever as this."

"Oh, you can't take *me* in!"

"No. . . . Well, I was wondering about this ghost of yours, Bill. It seems to me——"

"Oh, *that!*" Bill was profoundly disappointed. "What on earth has the ghost got to do with it?"

"I don't know," said Antony apologetically. "I don't know what anything has got to do with it. I was just wondering. You shouldn't have brought me here if you hadn't wanted me to think about the ghost. This is where she appeared, isn't it?"

"Yes." Bill was distinctly short about it.

"How?"

"What?"

"I said, 'How?' "

"How? How *do* ghosts appear? I don't know. They just appear."

"Over four or five hundred yards of open park?"

"Well, but she had to appear here, because this is

where the original one—Lady Anne, you know—was supposed to walk."

"Oh, never mind Lady Anne! A real ghost can do anything. But how did Miss Norris appear suddenly—over five hundred yards of bare park?"

Bill looked at Antony with open mouth.

"I—I don't know," he stammered. "We never thought of that."

"You would have seen her long before, wouldn't you, if she had come the way *we* came?"

"Of course we should."

"And that would have spoilt it rather. You would have had time to recognize her walk."

Bill was interested now.

"That's rather funny, you know, Tony. We none of us thought of that."

"You're sure she didn't come across the park when none of you were looking?"

"Quite. Because, you see, Betty and I were expecting her, and we kept looking round in case we saw her, so that we should all be playing with our backs to her.

"You and Miss Calladine were playing together?"

"I say, however do you know that?"

"Brilliant deductive reasoning. Well, then you suddenly saw her?"

"Yes, she walked across that side of the lawn." He indicated the opposite side, nearer to the house.

"She couldn't have been hiding in the ditch? Do you call it the moat, by the way?"

"Mark does. We don't among ourselves. No, she couldn't. Betty and I were here before the others, and walked round a bit. We should have seen her."

"Then she must have been hiding in the shed. Or do you call it the summer-house?"

"We had to go there for the bowls, of course. She couldn't have been there."

"Oh!"

"It's dashed funny," said Bill, after an interval for thought. "But it doesn't matter, does it? It has nothing to do with Robert."

"Hasn't it?"

"I say, *has* it?" said Bill, getting excited again.

"I don't know. We don't know what has, or what hasn't. But it *has* got something to do with Miss Norris. And Miss Norris——" He broke off suddenly.

"What about her?"

"Well, you're all in it in a kind of way. And if something unaccountable happens to one of you a day or two before something unaccountable happens to the whole house, one is—well, interested." It was a good enough reason, but it wasn't the reason he had been on the point of giving.

"I see. Well?"

Antony knocked out his pipe and got up slowly.

"Well then, let's find the way from the house by which Miss Norris came."

Bill jumped up eagerly.

"By Jove! Do you mean there's a secret passage?"

"A secluded passage, anyway. There must be."

"I say, what fun! I love secret passages. Good Lord, and this afternoon I was playing golf just like an ordinary merchant! What a life! Secret passages!"

They made their way down into the ditch. If an opening was to be found which led to the house, it would probably be on the house side of the green, and on the outside of the ditch. The most obvious place at which to begin the search was the shed where the bowls were kept. It was a tidy place—as anything in Mark's establishment would be. There were two boxes of croquet things, one of them with the lid open, as if the balls and mallets and hoops (neatly enough put away, though) had been recently used; a box of bowls, a small lawn-mower, a roller and so forth. A seat ran along the back of it, whereon the bowls-players could sit when it rained.

Antony tapped the wall at the back.

"This is where the passage ought to begin. It doesn't sound very hollow, does it?"

"It needn't begin here at all, need it?" said Bill, walking round with bent head, and tapping the other walls. He was just too tall to stand upright in the shed.

"There's only one reason why it should, and that is that it would save us the trouble of looking anywhere else for it. Surely Mark didn't let you play croquet on his bowling-green?" He pointed to the croquet things.

"He didn't encourage it at one time, but this year he got rather keen about it. There's really nowhere else to play. Personally I hate the game. He wasn't very keen on bowls, you know, but he liked calling it the bowling-green, and surprising his visitors with it."

Antony laughed.

"I love you on Mark," he said. "You're priceless."

He began to feel in his pockets for his pipe and tobacco, and then suddenly stopped and stiffened to attention. For a moment he stood listening, with his head on one side, holding up a finger to bid Bill listen too.

"What is it?" whispered Bill.

Antony waved him to silence, and remained listening. Very quietly he went down on his knees, and listened again. Then he put his ear to the floor. He got up and dusted himself quickly, walked across to Bill and whispered in his ear:

"Footsteps. Somebody coming. When I begin to talk, back me up.

Bill nodded. Antony gave him an encouraging pat on the back, and stepped firmly across to the box of bowls, whistling loudly to himself. He took the bowls out, dropped one with a loud bang on the floor, said, "Oh, Lord!" and went on:

"I say, Bill, I don't think I want to play bowls, after all."

"Well, why did you say you did?" grumbled Bill.

Antony flashed a smile of appreciation at him.

"Well, I wanted to when I said I did, and now I don't want to."

"Then what *do* you want to do?"

"Talk."

"Oh, right-*o!*" said Bill eagerly.

"There's a seat on the law—I saw it. Let's bring these things along in case we want to play, after all."

"Right-o!" said Bill again. He felt safe with that, not wishing to commit himself until he knew what he was wanted to say.

As they went across the lawn, Antony dropped the bowls and took out his pipe.

"Got a match?" he said loudly.

As he bent his head over the match, he whispered, "There'll be somebody listening to us. You take the Cayley view," and then went on in his ordinary voice, "I don't think much of your matches, Bill," and struck another. They walked over to the seat and sat down.

"What a heavenly night!" said Antony.

"Ripping."

"I wonder where that poor devil Mark is now."

"It's a rum business."

"You agree with Cayley—that it was an accident?"

"Yes. You see, I know Mark."

"H'm." Antony produced a pencil and a piece of paper and began to write on his knee, but while he wrote, he talked. He said that he thought Mark had shot his brother in a fit of anger, and that Cayley knew, or anyhow guessed, this, and had tried to give his cousin a chance of getting away.

"Mind you, I think he's right. I think it's what any of us would do. I shan't give it away, of course, but somehow there are one or two little things which make me think that Mark really did shoot his brother —I mean other than accidentally."

"Murdered him?"

"Well, manslaughtered him, anyway. I may be wrong. Anyway, it's not my business."

"But why do you think so? Because of the keys?"

"Oh, the keys are a wash-out. Still, it was a brilliant idea of mine, wasn't it? And it would have been rather a score for me if they *had* all been outside."

He had finished his writing, and now passed the paper over to Bill. In the clear moonlight the carefully printed letters could easily be read:

"GO ON TALKING AS IF I WERE HERE. AFTER A MINUTE OR TWO, TURN ROUND AS IF I WERE SITTING ON THE GRASS BEHIND YOU, BUT GO ON TALKING."

"I know you don't agree with me," Antony went on as Bill read, "but you'll see that I'm right."

Bill looked up and nodded eagerly. He had forgotten golf and Betty and all the other things which had made up his world lately. This was the real thing. This was life.

"Well," he began deliberately, "the whole point is that I know Mark. Now, Mark——"

But Antony was off the seat and letting himself gently down into the ditch. His intention was to crawl round it until the shed came in sight. The footsteps which he had heard seemed to be underneath the shed; probably there was a trap-door of some kind in the floor. Whoever it was would have heard their voices, and would probably think it worth while to listen to what they were saying. He might do this merely by opening the door a little without showing himself, in which case Antony would have found the entrance to the passage without any trouble to himself. But when Bill turned his head and talked over the back of the seat, it was probable that the listener would find it necessary to put his head outside in order to hear, and then Antony would be able to discover who it was. Moreover, if he should venture out of his hiding-place altogether and peep at them over the top of the bank, the fact that Bill was talking over the back of the seat would mislead the watcher into thinking that Antony was still there, sitting on the grass, no doubt, behind the seat, swinging his legs over the side of the ditch.

He walked quickly but very silently along the half-length of the bowling-green to the first corner, passed cautiously round, and then went even more carefully along the width of it to the second corner. He could hear Bill hard at it, arguing from his knowledge of Mark's character that this, that and the other must have happened, and he smiled appreciatively to himself. Bill was a great conspirator—worth a hundred Watsons. As he approached the second corner he slowed down, and did the last few yards on hands and knees. Then, lying at full length, inch by inch his head went round the corner.

The shed was two or three yards to his left, on the opposite side of the ditch. From where he lay he could see almost entirely inside it. Everything seemed to be as they left it. The bowls-box, the lawn-mower, the roller, the open croquet-box, the——

"By Jove!" said Antony to himself, "that's neat."

The lid of the other croquet-box was open, too.

Bill was turning round now; his voice became more difficult to hear. "You see what I mean," he was saying. "If Cayley——"

And out of the second croquet-box came Cayley's black head.

Antony wanted to shout his applause. It was neat, devilish neat. For a moment he gazed, fascinated, at that wonderful new kind of croquet-ball which had appeared so dramatically out of the box, and then reluctantly wriggled himself back. There was nothing to be gained by staying there, and a good deal to be lost, for Bill showed signs of running down. As quickly as he could Antony hurried round the ditch and took up his place at the back of the seat. Then he stood up with a yawn, stretched himself and said carelessly, "Well, don't worry yourself about it, Bill, old man. I daresay you're right. You know Mark, and I don't; and that's the difference. Shall we have a game or shall we go to bed?"

Bill looked at him for inspiration, and, receiving it, said, "Oh, just let's have one game, shall we?"

"Right you are," said Antony.

But Bill was much too excited to take the game which followed very seriously. Antony, on the other hand, seemed to be thinking of nothing but bowls.

He played with great deliberation for ten minutes, and then announced that he was going to bed. Bill looked at him anxiously.

"It's all right," laughed Antony. "You can talk if you want to. Just let's put 'em away first, though."

They made their way down to the shed, and while Bill was putting the bowls away, Antony tried the lid of the closed croquet-box. As he expected, it was locked.

"Now then," said Bill, as they were walking back to the house again, "I'm simply bursting to know. Who was it?"

"Cayley."

"Good Lord! Where?"

"Inside one of the croquet-boxes."

"Don't be an ass."

"It's quite true, Bill." He told the other what he had seen.

"But aren't we going to have a look at it?" asked Bill, in great disappointment. "I'm longing to explore, Aren't you?"

"To-morrow and to-morrow and to-morrow. We shall see Cayley coming along this way directly. Besides, I want to get in from the other end, if I can. I doubt very much if we can do it this end without giving ourselves away. . . . Look, there's Cayley."

They could see him coming along the drive towards them. When they were a little closer, they waved to him and he waved back.

"I wondered where you were," he said, as he got up to them. "I rather thought you might be along this way. What about bed?"

"We've been playing bowls," added Bill, "and talking, and—and playing bowls. Ripping night, isn't it?"

But he left the rest of the conversation, as they

wandered back to the house, to Antony. He wanted
to think. There seemed to be no doubt now that
Cayley was a villain. Bill had never been familiar
with a villain before. It didn't seem quite fair of
Cayley, somehow; he was taking a mean advantage
of his friends. Lot of funny people there were in the
world—funny people with secrets. Look at Tony, that
first time he had met him in a tobacconist's shop. Anybody would have thought he was a tobacconist's assistant. And Cayley. Anybody would have thought
that Cayley was an ordinary decent sort of person.
And Mark. Dash it! one could never be sure of anybody. Now, Robert was different. Everybody had always said that Robert was a shady fellow. . . .

But what on earth had Miss Norris got to do with
it?

What had Miss Norris got to do with it? This was
a question which Antony had already asked himself
that afternoon, and it seemed to him now that he
had found the answer. As he lay in bed that night he
reassembled his ideas, and looked at them in the new
light which the events of the evening threw upon the
dark corners in his brain.

Of course it was natural that Cayley should want
to get rid of his guests as soon as the tragedy was
discovered. He would want this for their own sake
as well as for his. But he had been a little too quick
about suggesting it, and about seeing the suggestion
carried out. They had been bustled off as soon as they
could be packed. The suggestion that they were in his
hands, to go or stay as he wished, could have been
left safely to them. As it was, they had been given no
alternative, and Miss Norris, who had proposed to
catch an after-dinner train at the junction, in the
obvious hope that she might have in this a dramatic

cross-examination at the hands of some keen-eyed detective, was encouraged tactfully, but quite firmly, to travel by the earlier train with the others. Antony had felt that Cayley, in the tragedy which had suddenly befallen the house, ought to have been equally indifferent to her presence or absence. But he was not; and Antony assumed from this that Cayley was very much alive to the necessity for her absence.

Why?

Well, that question was not to be answered off-hand. But the fact that it was so had made Antony interested in her; and it was for this reason that he had followed up so alertly Bill's casual mention of her in connexion with the dressing-up business. He felt that he wanted to know a little more about Miss Norris and the part she had played in the Red House circle. By sheer luck, as it seemed to him, he had stumbled on the answer to his question.

Miss Norris was hurried away because she knew about the secret passage.

The passage, then, had something to do with the mystery of Robert's death. Miss Norris had used it in order to bring off her dramatic appearance as the ghost. Possibly she had discovered it for herself; possibly Mark had revealed it to her secretly one day, never guessing that she would make so unkind a use of it later on; possibly Cayley, having been let into the joke of the dressing-up, had shown her how she could make her appearance on the bowling-green even more mysterious and supernatural. One way or another, she knew about the secret passage. So she must be hurried away.

Why? Because if she stayed and talked, she might make some innocent mention of it. And Cayley did not want any mention of it.

Why, again? Obviously because the passage, or even the mere knowledge of its existence, might provide a clue.

"I wonder if Mark's hiding there," thought Antony; and he went to sleep.

CHAPTER X

MR. GILLINGHAM TALKS NONSENSE

Antony came down in a very good humour to breakfast next morning, and found that his host was before him. Cayley looked up from his letters and nodded.

"Any word of Mr. Ablett—of Mark?" said Antony, at he poured out his coffee.

"No. The inspector wants to drag the lake this afternoon."

"Oh! Is there a lake?"

There was just the flicker of a smile on Cayley's face, but it disappeared as quickly as it came.

"Well, it's really a pond," he said, "but it was called 'the lake.'"

"By Mark," thought Antony. Aloud he said, "What do they expect to find?"

"They think that Mark——" He broke off and shrugged his shoulders.

"May have drowned himself, knowing that he couldn't get away? And knowing that he had compromised himself by trying to get away at all?"

"Yes; I suppose so," said Cayley slowly.

"I should have thought he would have given himself more of a run for his money. After all, he had a revolver. If he was determined not to be taken alive, he could always have prevented that. Couldn't he

have caught a train to London before the police
knew anything about it?"

"He might just have managed it. There *was* a
train. They would have noticed him at Woodham,
of course, but he might have managed it at Stanton.
He's not so well-known there, naturally. The inspector
has been inquiring. Nobody seems to have seen him."

"There are sure to be people who will say they
did, later on. There was never a missing man yet
but a dozen people come forward who swear to have
seen him at a dozen different places at the same time."

Cayley smiled.

"Yes. That's true. Anyhow, he wants to drag the
pond first." He added dryly, "From what I've read
of detective stories, inspectors always do want to drag
the pond first."

"Is it deep?"

"Quite deep enough," said Cayley as he got up.
On his way to the door he stopped, and looked at
Antony. "I'm so sorry that we're keeping you here
like this, but it will only be until to-morrow. The
inquest is to-morrow afternoon. Do amuse yourself
how you like till then. Beverley will look after you."

"Thanks very much. I shall really be quite all
right."

Antony went on with his breakfast. Perhaps it
was true that inspectors liked dragging ponds, but
the question was, Did Cayleys like having them
dragged? Was Cayley anxious about it, or quite indifferent? He certainly did not seem to be anxious,
but he could hide his feelings very easily beneath that
heavy, solid face, and it was not often that the real
Cayley peeped out. Just a little too eager once or
twice perhaps, but there was nothing to be learnt
from it this morning. Perhaps he knew that the pond

had no secrets to give up. After all, inspectors were always dragging ponds.

Bill came in noisily.

Bill's face was an open book. Excitement was written all over it.

"Well," he said eagerly, as he sat down to the business of the meal, "what are we going to do this morning?"

"Not talk so loudly, for one thing," said Antony.

Bill looked about him apprehensively. Was Cayley under the table, for example? After last night one never knew.

"Is—er——" He raised his eyebrows.

"No. But one doesn't want to shout. One should modulate the voice, my dear William, while breathing gently from the hips. Thus one avoids those chest-notes which have betrayed many a secret. In other words, pass the toast."

"You seem bright this morning."

"I am. Very bright. Cayley noticed it. Cayley said, 'Were it not that I have other business, I would come gathering nuts and may with thee. Fain would I gyrate round the mulberry-bush and hop upon the little hills. But the waters of Jordan encompass me and Inspector Birch tarries outside with his shrimping-net. My friend William Beverley will attend thee anon. Farewell, a long farewell to all thy grape-nuts.' He then left up-centre. Enter W. Beverley, R."

"Are you often like this at breakfast?"

"Almost invariably. Said he with his mouth full. Exit W. Beverley, L."

"It's a touch of the sun, I suppose," said Bill, shaking his head sadly.

"It's the sun and the moon and the stars, all acting together on an empty stomach. Do you know

anything about the stars, Mr. Beverley? Do you
know anything about Orion's Belt, for instance?
And why isn't there a star called Beverley's Belt? Or
a novel? Said he masticating. Re-enter W. Beverley
through trap-door."

"Talking about trap-doors——"

"Don't" said Antony, getting up. "Some talk of
Alexander and some of Hercules, but nobody talks
about—what's the Latin for trap-door? *Mensa*—a table;
you might get it from that. Well, Mr. Beverley,"—
and he slapped him heartily on the back as he went
past him—"I shall see you later. Cayley says that you
will amuse me, but so far you have not made me
laugh once. You must try and be more amusing when
you have finished your breakfast. But don't hurry.
Let the upper mandibles have time to do the work.
With those words Mr. Gillingham then left the
spacious apartment."

Bill continued his breakfast with a slightly bewildered air. He did not know that Cayley was
smoking a cigarette outside the windows behind him;
not listening, perhaps; possibly not even overhearing;
but within sight of Antony, who was not going to
take any risks. So he went on with his breakfast, re-
flecting that Antony was a rum fellow, and wondering if he had only dreamed of the amazing things
which had happened the day before.

Antony went up to his bedroom to fetch his pipe.
It was occupied by a housemaid, and he made a
polite apology for disturbing her. Then he remembered.

"Is it Elsie?" he asked, giving her a friendly smile.

"Yes, sir," she said, shy but proud. She had no
doubts as to why it was that she had achieved such
notoriety.

"It was you who heard Mr. Mark yesterday, wasn't it? I hope the inspector was nice to you?"

"Yes, thank you, sir."

"'It's *my* turn now. You wait,'" murmured Antony to himself.

"Yes, sir. Nasty-like. Meaning to say his chance had come."

"I wonder."

"Well, that's what I heard, sir. Truly."

Antony looked at her thoughtfully and nodded.

"Yes. I wonder. I wonder why."

"Why what, sir?"

"Oh, lots of things, Elsie. . . . It was quite an accident your being outside just then?"

Elsie blushed. She had not forgotten what Mrs. Stevens had said about it.

"Quite, sir. In the general way I use the other stairs."

"Of course."

He had found his pipe and was about to go downstairs again when she stopped him.

"I beg your pardon, sir, but will there be an inquest?"

"Oh, yes. To-morrow, I think."

"Shall I have to give my evidence, sir?"

"Of course. There's nothing to be frightened of, you know."

"I did hear it, sir. Truly."

"Why, of course you did. Who says you didn't?"

"Some of the others, sir—Mrs. Stevens and all."

"Oh, that's just because they're jealous," said Antony with a smile.

He was glad to have spoken to her, because he had recognized at once the immense importance of her evidence. To the inspector no doubt it had seemed only of importance in that it had shown Mark to have adopted something of a threatening attitude towards his brother. To Antony it had much more significance. It was the only trustworthy evidence that Mark had been in the office at all that afternoon.

For who saw Mark go into the office? Only Cayley. And if Cayley had been hiding the truth about the keys, why should he not be hiding the truth about Mark's entry into the office? Obviously all Cayley's evidence went for nothing. Some of it no doubt was true; but he was giving it, both truth and falsehood, with a purpose. What the purpose was Antony did not know as yet; to shield Mark, to shield himself, even to betray Mark—it might be any of these. But since his evidence was given for his own ends, it was impossible that it could be treated as the evidence of an impartial and trustworthy onlooker. Such, for instance, as Elsie appeared to be.

Elsie's evidence, however, seemed to settle the point. Mark had gone into the office to see his brother; Elsie had heard them both talking; and then Antony and Cayley had found the body of Robert . . . and the inspector was going to drag the pond.

But certainly Elsie's evidence did not prove anything more than the mere presence of Mark in the room. "It's my turn now; you wait." That was not an immediate threat; it was a threat for the future. If Mark had shot his brother immediately afterwards it must have been an accident, the result of a struggle, say, provoked by that "nasty-like" tone of voice. Nobody would say "You wait" to a man who was just going to be shot. "You wait" meant "You wait, and see what's going to happen to you later on." The owner of the Red House had had enough of his brother's sponging, his brother's blackmail; now it was Mark's turn to get a bit of his own back. Let Robert just wait a bit, and he would see. The conversation which Elsie had overheard might have meant something like this. It couldn't have meant murder. Anyway not murder of Robert by Mark.

"It's a funny business," thought Antony. "The one obvious solution is so easy and yet so wrong. And I've got a hundred things in my head, and I can't fit them together. And this afternoon will make a hundred and one. I mustn't forget this afternoon."

He found Bill in the hall and proposed a stroll. Bill was only too ready.

"Where do you want to go?" he asked.

"I don't mind much. Show me the park."

"Righto."

They walked out together.

"Watson, old man," said Antony, as soon as they were away from the house, "you really mustn't talk so loudly indoors. There was a gentleman outside, just behind you, all the time."

"Oh, I say," said Bill, going pink. "I'm awfully sorry. So that's why you were talking such rot."

"Partly, yes. And partly because I do feel rather bright this morning. We're going to have a busy day."

"Are we really? What are we going to do?"

"They're going to drag the pond—beg its pardon, the lake. Where *is* the lake?"

"We're on the way to it now, if you'd like to see it."

"We may as well look at it. Do you haunt the lake much in the ordinary way?"

"Oh, no, rather not. There's nothing to do there."

"You can't bathe?"

"Well, I shouldn't care to. Too dirty."

"I see. . . . This is the way we came yesterday, isn't it? The way to the village?"

"Yes. We go off a bit to the right directly. What are they dragging it for?"

"Mark."

"Oh, rot," said Bill uneasily. He was silent for a little, and then, forgetting his uncomfortable thoughts in his sudden remembrance of the exciting times they were having, said eagerly, "I say, when are we going to look for that passage?"

"We can't do very much while Cayley's in the house."

"What about this afternoon when they're dragging the pond? He's sure to be there."

Antony shook his head.

"There's something I *must* do this afternoon," he said. "Of course we might have time for both."

"Has Cayley got to be out of the house for the other thing too?"

"Well, I think he ought to be."

"I say, is it anything rather exciting?"

"I don't know. It might be rather interesting. I daresay I could do it at some other time, but I rather fancy it at three o'clock, somehow. I've been specially keeping it back for then."

"I say, what fun! You *do* want me, don't you?"

"Of course I do. Only, Bill—don't talk about things *i*nside the house, unless I begin. There's a good Watson."

"I won't. I swear I won't."

They had come to the pond—Mark's lake—and they walked silently round it. When they had made the circle, Antony sat down on the grass, and relit his pipe. Bill followed his example.

"Well, Mark isn't there," said Antony.

"No," said Bill. "At least, I don't quite see why you know he isn't."

"It isn't 'knowing,' it's 'guessing,'" said Antony rapidly. "It's much easier to shoot yourself than to drown yourself, and if Mark had wanted to shoot himself in the water, with some idea of not letting the body be found, he'd have put big stones in his pockets, and the only big stones are near the water's edge, and they would have left marks, and they haven't, and therefore he didn't, and—oh, bother the pond; that can wait till this afternoon. Bill, where does the secret passage begin?"

"Well, that's what we've got to find out, isn't it?"

"Yes. You see, my idea is this."

He explained his reasons for thinking that the secret of the passage was concerned in some way with the secret of Robert's death, and went on:

"My theory is that Mark discovered the passage about a year ago—the time when he began to get keen on croquet. The passage came out into the floor of the shed, and probably it was Cayley's idea to put a croquet-box over the trap-door, so as to hide it more completely. You know, when once you've discovered a secret yourself, it always seems as if it must be so obvious to everybody else. I can imagine that Mark loved having this little secret all to himself—and to Cayley, of course, but Cayley wouldn't count—and they must have had great fun fixing it up, and making it more difficult for other people to find out. Well, then, when Miss Norris was going to dress-up, Cayley gave it away. Probably he told her that she could never get down to the bowling-green without being discovered, and then perhaps showed that he knew there was one way in which she could

do it, and she wormed the secret out of him somehow."

"But this was two or three days before Robert
turned up."

"Exactly. I am not suggesting that there was anything sinister about the passage in the first place. It
was just a little private bit of romance and adventure
for Mark, three days ago. He didn't even know that
Robert was coming. But somehow the passage has
been used since, in connexion with Robert. Perhaps
Mark escaped that way; perhaps he's hiding there
now. And if so, then the only person who could give
him away was Miss Norris. And she of course could
only do it innocently—not knowing that the passage
had anything to do with it."

"So it was safer to have her out of the way?"

"Yes."

"But, look here, Tony, why do you want to bother
about *this* end of it? We can always get in at the
bowling-green end."

"I know, but if we do that we shall have to do it
openly. It will mean breaking open the box, and
letting Cayley know that we've done it. You see, Bill,
if we don't find anything out for ourselves in the
next day or two, we've got to tell the police what
we *have* found out, and then they can explore the
passage for themselves. But I don't want to do that
yet."

"Rather not."

"So we've got to carry on secretly for a bit. It's
the only way." He smiled and added, "And it's
much more fun."

"Rather!" Bill chuckled to himself.

"Very well, then. Where does the secret passage
begin?"

CHAPTER XI

THE REVEREND THEODORE USSHER

"There's one thing which we have got to realize at once," said Antony, "and that is that if we don't find it easily, we shan't find it at all."

"You mean that we shan't have time?"

"Neither time nor opportunity. Which is rather a consoling thought to a lazy person like me."

"But it makes it much harder, if we can't really look properly."

"Harder to find, yes, but so much easier to look. For instance, the passage might begin in Cayley's bedroom. Well, now we know that it doesn't."

"We don't know anything of the sort," protested Bill.

"We know for the purposes of our search. Obviously we can't go trailing into Cayley's bedroom and tapping his wardrobes; and obviously, therefore, if we are going to look for it at all, we must assume that it doesn't begin there."

"Oh, I see." Bill chewed a piece of grass thoughtfully. "Anyhow, it wouldn't begin on an upstairs floor, would it?"

"Probably not. Well, we're getting on."

"You can wash out the kitchen and all that part of the house," said Bill, after more thought. "We can't go there."

"Right. And the cellars, if there are any."

"Well, that doesn't leave us much."

"No. Of course it's only a hundred-to-one chance that we find it, but what we want to consider is which is the most likely place of the few places in which we can look safely."

"All it amounts to," said Bill, "is the living-rooms downstairs—dining-room, library, hall, billiard-room and the office rooms."

"Yes, that's all."

"Well, the office is the most likely, isn't it?"

"Yes. Except for one thing."

"What's that?"

"Well, it's on the wrong side of the house. One would expect the passage to start from the nearest place to which it is going. Why make it longer by going under the house first?"

"Yes, that's true. Well, then, you think the dining-room or the library?"

"Yes. And the library for choice. I mean for *our* choice. There are always servants going into dining-rooms. We shouldn't have much of a chance of exploring properly in there. Besides, there's another thing to remember. Mark has kept this a secret for a year. Could he have kept it a secret in the dining-room? Could Miss Norris have got into the dining-room and used the secret door just after dinner without being seen? It would have been much too risky."

Bill got up eagerly.

"Come along," he said, "let's try the library. If Cayley comes in, we can always pretend we're choosing a book."

Antony got up slowly, took his arm and walked back to the house with him.

The library was worth going into, passages or no

passages. Antony could never resist another person's bookshelves. As soon as he went into the room, he found himself wandering round it to see what books the owner read, or (more likely) did not read, but kept for the air which they lent to the house. Mark had prided himself on his library. It was a mixed collection of books. Books which he had inherited both from his father and from his patron; books which he had bought because he was interested in them, or if not in them, in the authors to whom he wished to lend his patronage; books which he had ordered in beautifully bound editions, partly because they looked well on his shelves, lending a noble colour to his rooms, partly because no man of culture should ever be without them; old editions, new editions, expensive books, cheap books—a library in which everybody, whatever his taste, could be sure of finding something to suit him.

"And which is *your* particular fancy, Bill?" said Antony, looking from one shelf to another. "Or are you always playing billiards?"

"I have a look at 'Badminton' sometimes," said Bill. "It's over in that corner there." He waved a hand.

"Over here?" said Antony, going to it.

"Yes." He corrected himself suddenly. "Oh, no, it's not. It's over there on the right now. Mark had a grand re-arrangement of his library about a year ago. It took him more than a week, he told us. He's got such a frightful lot, hasn't he?"

"Now that's very interesting," said Antony, and he sat down and filled his pipe again.

There was indeed a "frightful lot" of books. The four walls of the library were plastered with them from floor to ceiling, save only where the door and the two windows insisted on living their own life, even though an illiterate one. To Bill it seemed the most hopeless room of any in which to look for a secret opening.

"We shall have to take every blessed book down," he said, "before we can be certain that we haven't missed it."

"Anyway," said Antony, "if we take them down one at a time, nobody can suspect us of sinister designs. After all, what does one go into a library for, except to take books down?"

"But there's such a frightful lot."

Antony's pipe was now going satisfactorily, and he got up and walked leisurely to the end of the wall opposite the door.

"Well, let's have a look," he said, "and see if they *are* so very frightful. Hallo, here's your 'Badminton.' You often read that, you say?"

"If I read anything."

"Yes." He looked down and up the shelf. "Sport and Travel chiefly. I like books of travel, don't you?"

"They're pretty dull as a rule."

"Well, anyhow, some people like them very much," said Antony reproachfully. He moved on to the next row of shelves. "The Drama. The Restoration dramatists. Congreve. You can have Congreve. Still, as you well remark, Bill, many people think he's funny. Shaw, Wilde, Robertson—I like reading plays, Bill. There are not many people who do, but those who do are usually very keen. Let us pass on."

"I say, we haven't too much time," said Bill restlessly.

"We haven't. That's why we aren't wasting any. Poetry. Who reads nowadays? Bill, when did you last read 'Paradise Lost'?"

"Never."

"I thought not. And when did Miss Calladine last read 'The Excursion' aloud to you?"

"As a matter of fact, Betty—Miss Calladine—happens to be jolly keen on—what's the beggar's name?"

"Never mind his name. You have said quite enough. We pass on."

He moved on to the next shelf.

"Biography. Oh, lots of it. I love biographies. Are you a member of the Johnson Club? I bet Mark is. 'Memories of Many Courts'—I'm sure Mrs. Calladine reads that. Anyway, biographies are just as interesting as most novels, so why linger? We pass on." He went to the next shelf, and then gave a sudden whistle. "Hallo, hallo!"

"What's the matter?" said Bill rather peevishly.

"Stand back there. Keep the crowd back, Bill. We are getting amongst it. Sermons, as I live. Sermons. Was Mark's father a clergyman, or does Mark take to them naturally?"

"His father was a parson, I believe. Oh, yes, I know he was."

"Ah, then these are Father's books. 'Half-Hours with the Infinite'—I must order that from the library when I get back. 'The Lost Sheep,' 'Jones on the Trinity,' 'The Epistles of St. Paul Explained'—Oh, Bill, we're amongst it. 'The Narrow Way, being Sermons by the Rev. Theodore Ussher'—hal-*lo!*"

"What *is* the matter?"

"William, I am inspired. Stand by." He took down the Reverend Theodore Ussher's classic work, looked at it with a happy smile for a moment, and then gave it to Bill. "Here, hold Ussher for a bit."

Bill took the book obediently.

"No, give it me back. Just go out into the hall, and

see if you can hear Cayley anywhere. Say 'Hallo'
loudly, if you do."

Bill went out quickly, listened, and came back.

"It's all right."

"Good." He took the book out of its shelf again.
"Now then, you can hold Ussher. Hold him in the
left hand—so. With the right or dexter hand, grasp
this shelf firmly—so. Now, when I say 'Pull,' pull
gradually. Got that?"

Bill nodded, his face alight with excitement.

"Good." Antony put his hand into the space left
by the stout Ussher, and fingered the back of the
shelf. "Pull," he said.

Bill pulled.

"Now just go on pulling like that. I shall get it directly. Not hard, you know, but just keeping up the
strain." His fingers went at it again busily. . . .

And then suddenly the whole row of shelves, from
top to bottom, swung gently open towards them.

"Good Lord!" said Bill, letting go of the shelf in
his amazement.

Antony pushed the shelves back, extracted Ussher
from Bill's fingers, replaced him, and then, taking
Bill by the arm, led him to the sofa and deposited
him in it. Standing in front of him, he bowed gravely.

"Child's play, Watson," he said; "child's play."

"How on earth——"

Antony laughed happily and sat down on the sofa
beside him.

"You don't really want it explained," he said,
smacking him on the knee; "you're just being Watsonish. It's very nice of you, of course, and I ap-
preciate it."

"No, but really, Tony."

"Oh, my dear Bill!" He smoked silently for a little, and then went on, "It's what I was saying just now—a secret is a secret until you have discovered it, and as soon as you have discovered it, you wonder why everybody else isn't discovering it, and how it could ever have been a secret at all. This passage has been here for years, with an opening at one end into the library, and at the other end into the shed. Then Mark discovered it, and immediately he felt that everybody else must discover it. So he made the shed end more difficult by putting the croquet-box there, and this end more difficult by——" he stopped and looked at the other—"by what, Bill?"

But Bill was being Watsonish.

"What?"

"Obviously by re-arranging his books. He happened to take out 'The Life of Nelson' or 'Three Men in a Boat,' or whatever it was, and by the merest chance discovered the secret. Naturally he felt that everybody else would be taking down 'The Life of Nelson' or 'Three Men in a Boat.' Naturally he felt that the secret would be safer if nobody ever interfered with that shelf at all. When you said that the books had been re-arranged a year ago—just about the time the croquet-box came into existence—of course I guessed why. So I looked about for the dullest books I could find, the books nobody ever read. Obviously the collection of sermon-books of a mid-Victorian clergyman was the shelf we wanted."

"Yes, I see. But why were you so certain of the particular place?"

"Well, he had to mark the particular place by *some* book. I thought that the joke of putting "The Narrow Way' just over the entrance to the passage might appeal to him. Apparently it did."

Bill nodded to himself thoughtfully several times. "Yes, that's very neat," he said. "You're a clever devil, Tony."

Tony laughed.

"You encourage me to think so, which is bad for me, but very delightful."

"Well, come on, then," said Bill, and he got up, and held out a hand.

"Come on where?"

"To explore the passage, of course."

Antony shook his head.

"Why ever not?"

"Well, what do you expect to find there?"

"I don't know. But you seemed to think that we might find something that would help."

"Suppose we find Mark?" said Antony quietly.

"I say, do you really think he's there?"

"Suppose he is?"

"Well, then, there we are."

Antony walked over to the fireplace, knocked out the ashes of his pipe, and turned back to Bill. He looked at him gravely without speaking.

"What are you going to say to him?" he said at last.

"How do you mean?"

"Are you going to arrest him, or help him to escape?"

"I—I—well, of course, I——" began Bill, stammering, and then ended lamely, "Well, I don't know."

"Exactly. We've got to make up our minds, haven't we?"

Bill didn't answer. Very much disturbed in his mind, he walked restlessly about the room, frowning to himself, stopping now and then at the newly discovered door and looking at it as if he were trying to learn what lay behind it. Which side was he on, if it came to choosing sides—Mark's or the Law's?

"You know, you can't just say, 'Oh—er—hallo!' to him," said Antony, breaking rather appropriately into his thoughts.

Bill looked up at him with a start.

"Nor," went on Antony, "can you say, 'This is my friend Mr. Gillingham, who is staying with you. We were just going to have a game of bowls.'"

"Yes, it's dashed difficult. I don't know what to say. I've been rather forgetting about Mark." He wandered over to the window and looked out on to the lawns. There was a gardener clipping the grass edges. No reason why the lawn should be untidy just because the master of the house had disappeared. It was going to be a hot day again. Dash it, of course he had forgotten Mark. How could he think of him as an escaped murderer, a fugitive from justice, when everything was going on just as it did yesterday, and the sun was shining just as it did when they all drove off to their golf, only twenty-four hours ago? How could he help feeling that this was not real tragedy, but merely a jolly kind of detective game that he and Antony were playing?

He turned back to his friend.

"All the same," he said, "you wanted to find the passage and now you've found it. Aren't you going into it at all?"

Antony took his arm.

"Let's go outside again," he said. "We can't go into it now, anyhow. It's too risky, with Cayley about. Bill, I feel like you—just a little bit frightened. But what I'm frightened of I don't quite know. Anyway, you want to go on with it, don't you?"

"Yes," said Bill firmly. "We must."

"Then we'll explore the passage this afternoon, if we get the chance. And if we don't get the chance, then we'll try it to-night."

They walked across the hall and out into the sunlight again.

"Do you really think we might find Mark hiding there?" asked Bill.

"It's possible," said Antony. "Either Mark or——" He pulled himself up quickly. "No," he murmured to himself, "I won't let myself think that—not yet, anyway. It's too horrible."

CHAPTER XII

A SHADOW ON THE WALL

In the twenty hours or so at his disposal Inspector Birch had been busy. He had telegraphed to London a complete description of Mark in the brown flannel suit which he had last been seen wearing; he had made inquiries at Stanton as to whether anybody answering to this description had been seen leaving by the 4:20; and though the evidence which had been volunteered to him had been inconclusive, it made it possible that Mark had indeed caught that train, and had arrived in London before the police at the other end had been ready to receive him. But the fact that it was market-day at Stanton, and that the little town would be more full than usual of visitors, made it less likely that either the departure of Mark by the 4:20, or the arrival of Robert by the 2:10 earlier in the afternoon, would have been particularly noticed. As Antony had said to Cayley, there would always be somebody ready to hand the police a circumstantial story of the movments of any man in whom the police were interested.

That Robert had come by the 2:10 seemed fairly certain. To find out more about him in time for the inquest would be difficult. All that was known about him in the village where he and Mark had lived as boys bore out the evidence of Cayley. He was an unsatisfactory son, and he had been hurried off to Australia; nor had he been seen since in the village. Whether there were any more substantial grounds of quarrel between the two brothers than that the younger one was at home and well-to-do, while the elder was poor and an exile, was not known, nor, as far as the inspector could see, was it likely to be known until Mark was captured.

The discovery of Mark was all that mattered immediately. Dragging the pond might not help towards this, but it would certainly give the impression in court to-morrow that Inspector Birch was handling the case with zeal. And if only the revolver with which the deed was done was brought to the surface, his trouble would be well repaid. "Inspector Birch produces the weapon" would make an excellent headline in the local paper.

He was feeling well-satisfied with himself, therefore, as he walked to the pond, where his men were waiting for him, and quite in the mood for a little pleasant talk with Mr. Gillingham and his friend, Mr. Beverley. He gave them a cheerful "Good afternoon," and added with a smile, "Coming to help us?"

"You don't really want us," said Antony, smiling back at him.

"You can come if you like."

Antony gave a little shudder.

"You can tell me afterwards what you find," he said. "By the way," he added, "I hope the landlord at the 'George' gave me a good character?"

The inspector looked at him quickly.

"Now how on earth do you know anything about that?"

Antony bowed to him gravely.

"Because I guessed that you were a very efficient member of the Force."

The inspector laughed.

"Well, you came out all right, Mr. Gillingham. You got a clean bill. But I had to make certain about you."

"Of course you did. Well, I wish you luck. But I don't think you'll find much at the pond. It's rather out of the way, isn't it, for anybody running away?"

"That's just what I told Mr. Cayley, when he called my attention to the pond. However, we shan't do any harm by looking. It's the unexpected that's the most likely in this sort of case."

"You're quite right, Inspector. Well, we mustn't keep you. Good afternoon," and Antony smiled pleasantly at him.

"Good afternoon, sir."

"Good afternoon," said Bill.

Antony stood looking after the inspector as he strode off, silent for so long that Bill shook him by the arm at last, and asked him rather crossly what was the matter.

Antony shook his head slowly from side to side.

"I don't know; really I don't know. It's too devilish what I keep thinking. He can't be as cold-blooded as that."

"Who?"

Without answering, Antony led the way back to the garden-seat on which they had been sitting. He sat there with his head in his hands.

"Oh, I hope they find something," he murmured. "Oh, I hope they do."

"In the pond?"

"Yes."

"But what?"

"Anything, Bill; anything."

Bill was annoyed.

"I say, Tony, this won't do. You really mustn't be so damn mysterious. What's happened to you suddenly?"

Antony looked up at him in surprise.

"Didn't you hear what he said?"

"What, particularly?"

"That it was Cayley's idea to drag the pond."

"Oh! Oh, I say!" Bill was rather excited again. "You mean that he's hidden something there? Some false clue which he wants the police to find?"

"I hope so," said Antony earnestly, "but I'm afraid——" He stopped short.

"Afraid of what?"

"Afraid that he hasn't hidden anything there. Afraid that——"

"Well?"

"What's the safest place in which to hide anything very important?"

"Somewhere where nobody will look."

"There's a better place than that."

"What?"

"Somewhere where everybody has already looked."

"By Jove! You mean that as soon as the pond *has* been dragged, Cayley will hide something there?"

"Yes, I'm afraid so."

"But why afraid?"

"Because I think that it must be something very important, something which couldn't easily be hidden anywhere else."

"What?" asked Bill eagerly.

Antony shook his head.

"No, I'm not going to talk about it yet. We can

wait and see what the inspector finds. He may find something—I don't know what—something that Cayley has put there for him to find. But if he doesn't, then it will be because Cayley is going to hide something there to-night."

"What?" asked Bill again.

"You will see what, Bill," said Antony; "because we shall be there."

"Are we going to watch him?"

"Yes, if the inspector finds nothing."

"That's good," said Bill.

If it were a question of Cayley or the Law, he was quite decided as to which side he was taking. Previous to the tragedy of yesterday he had got on well enough with both of the cousins, without being in the least intimate with either. Indeed, of the two he preferred, perhaps, the silent, solid Cayley to the more volatile Mark. Cayley's qualities, as they appeared to Bill, may have been chiefly negative; but even if this merit lay in the fact that he never exposed whatever weaknesses he may have had, this is an excellent quality in a fellow-guest (or, if you like, fellow-host) in a house where one is continually visiting. Mark's weaknesses, on the other hand, were very plain to the eye, and Bill had seen a good deal of them.

Yet, though he had hesitated to define his position that morning in regard to Mark, he did not hesitate to place himself on the side of the Law against Cayley. Mark, after all, had done him no harm, but Cayley had committed an unforgivable offence. Cayley had listened secretly to a private conversation between himself and Tony. Let Cayley hang, if the Law demanded it.

Antony looked at his watch and stood up.

"Come along," he said. "It's time for that job I spoke about."

"The passage?" said Bill eagerly.

"No; the thing which I said that I had to do this afternoon."

"Oh, of course. What is it?"

Without saying anything, Antony led the way indoors to the office.

It was three o'clock, and at three o'clock yesterday Antony and Cayley had found the body. At a few minutes after three, he had been looking out of the window of the adjoining room, and had been surprised suddenly to find the door open and Cayley behind him. He had vaguely wondered at the time why he had expected the door to be shut, but he had had no time then to worry the thing out, and he had promised himself to look into it at his leisure afterwards. Possibly it meant nothing; possibly, if it meant anything, he could have found out its meaning by a visit to the office that morning. But he had felt that he would be more likely to recapture the impressions of yesterday if he chose as far as possible the same conditions for his experiment. So he had decided that three o'clock that afternoon should find him once more in the office.

As he went into the room, followed by Bill, he felt it almost as a shock that there was now no body of Robert lying there between the two doors. But there was a dark stain which showed where the dead man's head had been, and Antony knelt down over it, as he had knelt twenty-four hours before.

"I want to go through it again," he said. "You must be Cayley. Cayley said he would get some water. I remember thinking that water wasn't much good to a dead man, and that probably he was only too glad to do anything rather than nothing. He came back with a wet sponge and a handkerchief. I suppose he got the handkerchief from the chest of drawers. Wait a bit."

He got up and went into the adjoining room; looked round it, pulled open a drawer or two, and, after shutting all the doors, came back to the office.

"The sponge is there, and there are handkerchiefs in the top right-hand drawer. Now then, Bill, just pretend you're Cayley. You've just said something about water, and you get up."

Feeling that it was all a little uncanny, Bill, who had been kneeling beside his friend, got up and walked out. Antony, as he had done on the previous day, looked up after him as he went. Bill turned into the room on the right, opened the drawer and got the handkerchief, damped the sponge and came back.

"Well?" he said wonderingly.

Antony shook is head.

"It's all different," he said. "For one thing, you made a devil of a noise and Cayley didn't."

"Perhaps you weren't listening when Cayley went in?"

"I wasn't. But I should have heard him if I could have heard him, and I should have remembered afterwards."

"Perhaps Cayley shut the door after him."

"Wait!"

He pressed his hand over his eyes and thought. It wasn't anything which he had heard, but something which he had seen. He tried desperately hard to see it again. . . . He saw Cayley getting up, opening the door from the office, leaving it open and walking into the passage, turning to the door on the right, opening it, going in, and then—What did his eyes see after that? If they would only tell him again!

Suddenly he jumped up, his face alight. "Bill, I've got it!" he cried.

"What?"

"The shadow on the wall! I was looking at the shadow on the wall. Oh, ass, and ten times ass!"

Bill looked uncomprehendingly at him. Antony took his arm and pointed to the wall of the passage.

"Look at the sunlight on it," he said. "That's because you've left the door of that room open. The sun comes straight in through the windows. Now, I'm going to shut the door. Look! D'you see how the shadow moves across? That's what I saw—the shadow moving across as the door shut behind him. Bill, go in and shut the door behind you—quite naturally. Quick!"

Bill went out and Antony knelt, watching eagerly.

"I thought so!" he cried. "I knew it couldn't have been that."

"What happened?" said Bill, coming back.

"Just what you would expect. The sunlight came, and the shadow moved back again—all in one movement."

"And what happened yesterday?"

"The sunlight stayed there; and then the shadow came very slowly back, and there was no noise of the door being shut."

Bill looked at him with startled eyes.

"By Jove! You mean that Cayley closed the door afterwards—as an afterthought—and very quietly, so that you couldn't hear?"

Antony nodded.

"Yes. That explains why I was surprised afterwards when I went into the room to find the door open behind me. You know how those doors with springs on them close?"

"The sort which old gentlemen have to keep out draughts?"

"Yes. Just at first they hardly move at all, and then very, very slowly they swing to—well, that was the way the shadow moved, and subconsciously I must have associated it with the movement of that sort of door. By Jove!" He got up, and dusted his knees. "Now, Bill, just to make sure, go in and close the door like that. As an afterthought, you know; and very quietly, so that I don't hear the click of it."

Bill did as he was told, and then put his head out eagerly to hear what had happened.

"That was it," said Antony, with absolute conviction. "That was just what I saw yesterday." He came out of the office, and joined Bill in the little room.

"And now," he said, "let's try and find out what it was that Mr. Cayley was doing in here, and why he had to be so very careful that his friend Mr. Gillingham didn't overhear him."

CHAPTER XIII

THE OPEN WINDOW

Antony's first thought was that Cayley had hidden something; something, perhaps, which he had found by the body, and—but that was absurd. In the time at his disposal, he could have done no more than put it away in a drawer, where it would be much more open to discovery by Antony than if he had kept it in his pocket. In any case he would have removed it by this time, and hidden it in some more secret place. Besides, why in this case bother about shutting the door?

Bill pulled open a drawer in the chest, and looked inside.

"Is it any good going through these, do you think?" he asked.

Antony looked over his shoulder.

"Why did he keep clothes here at all?" he asked. "Did he ever change down here?"

"My dear Tony, he had more clothes than anybody in the world. He just kept them here in case they might be useful, I expect. When you and I go from London to the country we carry our clothes about with us. Mark never did. In his flat in London he had everything all over again which he has here. It was a hobby with him, collecting clothes. If he'd had half a dozen houses, they would all have been full of a complete gentleman's town and country outfit."

"I see."

"Of course, it might be useful sometimes, when he was busy in the next room, not to have to go upstairs for a handkerchief or a more comfortable coat."

"I see. Yes." He was walking round the room as he answered, and he lifted the top of the linen basket which stood near the wash basin and glanced in. "He seems to have come in here for a collar lately."

Bill peered in. There was one collar at the bottom of the basket.

"Yes. I daresay he would," he agreed. "If he suddenly found that the one he was wearing was uncomfortable or a little bit dirty, or something. He was very finicking."

Antony leant over and picked it out.

"It must have been uncomfortable this time," he said, after examining it carefully. "It couldn't very well be cleaner." He dropped it back again. "Anyway, he did come in here sometimes?"

"Oh, yes, rather."

"Yes, but what did Cayley come in for so secretly?"

"What did he want to shut the door for?" said Bill. "That's what I don't understand. You couldn't have seen him, anyhow."

"No. So it follows that I might have heard him. He was going to do something which he didn't want me to hear."

"By Jove, that's it!" said Bill eagerly.

"Yes; but what?"

Bill frowned hopefully to himself, but no inspiration came.

"Well, let's have some air, anyway," he said at last, exhausted by the effort, and he went to the window, opened it, and looked out. Then, struck by an idea, he turned back to Antony and said, "Do you think I had better go up to the pond to make sure that they're still at it? Because——" He broke off suddenly at the sight of Antony's face.

"Oh, idiot, idiot!" Antony cried. "Oh, most super-excellent of Watsons! Oh, you lamb, you blessing! Oh, Gillingham, you incomparable ass!"

"What on earth——"

"The window, the window!" cried Antony, point-ing to it.

Bill turned back to the window, expecting it to say something. As it said nothing, he looked at Antony again.

"He was opening the window!" cried Antony.

"Who?"

"Cayley, of course." Very gravely and slowly he expounded. "He came in here in order to open the window. He shut the door so that I shouldn't hear him open the window. He opened the window. I came in here and found the window open. I said, 'This window is open. My amazing powers of analy-sis tell me that the murderer must have escaped by this window.' 'Oh,' said Cayley, raising his eyebrows. 'Well,' said he, 'I suppose you must be right.' Said I proudly, 'I am. For the window is open,' I said. Oh, you incomparable ass!"

He understood now. It explained so much that had been puzzling him.

He tried to put himself in Cayley's place—Cayley, when Antony had first discovered him, hammering at the door and crying, "Let me in!" Whatever had happened inside the office, whoever had killed Rob-ert, Cayley knew all about it, and knew that Mark was not inside, and had not escaped by the window.

But it was necessary to Cayley's plans—to Mark's plans if they were acting in concert—that he should be thought so to have escaped. At some time, then, while he was hammering (the key in his pocket) at the locked door, he must suddenly have remembered —with what a shock!—that a mistake had been made. A window had not been left open!

Probably it would just have been a horrible doubt at first. *Was* the office window open?- Surely it was open! . . . *Was* it? . . . Would he have time now to unlock the door, slip in, open the French windows and slip out again? No. At any moment the servants might come. It was too risky. Fatal, if he were discovered. But servants were stupid. He could get the windows safely open while they were crowding round the body. They wouldn't notice. He could do it somehow.

And then Antony's sudden appearance! Here was a complication. And Antony suggesting that they should try the window! Why, the window was just what he wanted to avoid. No wonder he had seemed dazed at first.

Ah, and here at last was the explanation why they had gone the longest way round—and yet *run*. It was Cayley's only chance of getting a start on Antony, of getting to the windows first, of working them open somehow before Antony caught him up. Even if that were impossible, he must get there first, just to make sure. Perhaps they *were* open. He must get away from Antony and see. And if they were shut, hopelessly shut, then he must have a moment to himself, a moment in which to think of some other plan, and avoid the ruin which seemed so suddenly to be threatening.

So he had run. But Antony had kept up with him.

They had broken in the window together, and gone into the office. But Cayley was not done yet. There was the dressing-room window! But quietly, quietly. Antony mustn't hear.

And Antony didn't hear. Indeed, he had played up to Cayley splendidly. Not only had he called attention to the open window, but he had carefully explained to Cayley why Mark had chosen this particular window in preference to the office window. And Cayley had agreed that probably that was the reason. How he must have chuckled to himself! But he was still a little afraid. Afraid that Antony would examine the shrubbery. Why? Obviously because there was no trace of anyone having broken through the shrubbery. No doubt Cayley had provided the necessary traces since, and had helped the inspector to find them. Had he even gone as far as footmarks—in Mark's shoes? But the ground was very hard. Perhaps footmarks were not necessary. Antony smiled as he thought of the big Cayley trying to squeeze into the dapper little Mark's shoes. Cayley must have been glad that footmarks were not necessary.

No, the open window was enough; the open window and a broken twig or two. But quietly, quietly, Antony mustn't hear. And Antony had not heard. . . . But he had seen a shadow on the wall.

They were outside on the lawn again now. Bill and Antony, and Bill was listening open-mouthed to his friend's theory of yesterday's happenings. It fitted in, it explained things, but it did not get them any further. It only gave them another mystery to solve.

"What's that?" said Antony.

"Mark. Where's Mark? If he never went into the office at all, then where is he now?"

"I don't say that he never went into the office. In fact, he must have gone. Elsie heard him." He stopped and repeated slowly. "She heard him—at least she says she did. But if he was there, he came out again by the door."

"Well, but where does that lead you?"

"Where it led Mark. The passage."

"Do you mean that he's been hiding there all the time?"

Antony was silent until Bill had repeated his question, and then with an effort he came out of his thoughts and answered him.

"I don't know. But look here. Here is a possible explanation. I don't know if it is the right one—I don't know, Bill; I'm rather frightened. Frightened of what may have happened, of what may be going to happen. However, here is an explanation. See if you can find any fault with it."

With his legs stretched out and his hands deep in his pockets, he lay back on the garden-seat, looking up to the blue summer sky above him, and just as if he saw up there the events of yesterday being enacted over again, he described them slowly to Bill as they happened.

"We'll begin at the moment when Mark shoots Robert. Call it an accident; probably it was. Mark would say it was, anyhow. He is in a panic, naturally. But he doesn't lock the door and run away. For one thing, the key is on the outside of the door; for another, he is not quite such a fool as that. But he is in a horrible position. He is known to be on bad terms with his brother; he has just uttered some foolish threat to him, which may possibly have been overheard. What is he to do? He does the natural thing, the thing which Mark would always do in such circumstances. He consults Cayley, the invariable, inevitable Cayley.

"Cayley is just outside, Cayley must have heard the shot, Cayley will tell him what to do. He opens the door just as Cayley is coming to see what is the matter. He explains rapidly. 'What's to be done, Cay? what's to be done? It was an accident. I swear it was an accident. He threatened me. He would have shot me if I hadn't. Think of something, quick!'

"Cayley has thought of something. 'Leave it to me,' he says. 'You clear out altogether. *I* shot him, if you like. I'll do all the explaining. Get away. Hide. Nobody saw you go in. Into the passage, quick. I'll come to you there as soon as I can.'

"Good Cayley. Faithful Cayley! Mark's courage comes back. Cayley will explain all right. Cayley will tell the servants that it was an accident. He will ring up the police. Nobody will suspect Cayley—Cayley has no quarrel with Robert. And then Cayley will come into the passage and tell him that it is all right, and Mark will go out by the other end, and saunter slowly back to the house. He will be told the news by one of the servants. Robert accidentally shot? Good Heavens!

"So, greatly reassured, Mark goes into the library. And Cayley goes to the door of the office. . . . and locks it. And then bangs on the door and shouts, 'Let me in!'"

Antony was silent. Bill looked at him and shook his head.

"Yes, Tony, but that doesn't make sense. What's the point of Cayley behaving like that?"

Antony shrugged his shoulders without answering.

"And what has happened to Mark since?"

Antony shrugged his shoulders again.

"Well, the sooner we go into that passage, the better," said Bill.

"You're ready to go?"

"Quite," said Bill, surprised.

"You're quite ready for what we may find?"

"You're being dashed mysterious, old boy."

"I know I am." He gave a little laugh, and went on, "Perhaps I'm being an ass, just a melodramatic ass. Well, I hope I am." He looked at his watch.

"It's safe, is it? They're still busy at the pond?"

"We'd better make certain. Could you be a sleuth-hound, Bill—one of these that travel on their stomachs very noiselessly? I mean, could you get near enough to the pond to make sure that Cayley is still there, without letting him see you?"

"Rather!" He got up eagerly. "You wait."

Antony's head shot up suddenly. "Why, that was what Mark said," he cried.

"Mark?"

"Yes. What Elsie heard him say."

"Oh, that."

"Yes. . . . I suppose she couldn't have made a mistake, Bill? She did hear him?"

"She couldn't have mistaken his voice, if that's what you mean."

"Oh?"

"Mark had an extraordinarily characteristic voice."

"Oh!"

"Rather high-pitched, you know, and—well, one can't explain, but——"

"Yes?"

"Well, rather like this, you know, or even more so if anything." He rattled these words off in Mark's rather monotonous, high-pitched voice, and then laughed, and added in his natural voice, "I say, that was rather good."

Antony nodded quickly. "That was like it?" he said.

"Exactly."

"Yes." He got up and squeezed Bill's arm. "Well just go and see about Cayley, and then we'll get moving. I shall be in the library."

"Right."

Bill nodded and walked off in the direction of the pond. This was glorious fun; this was life. The immediate programme could hardly be bettered. First of all he was going to stalk Cayley. There was a little copse above the level of the pond, and about a hundred yards away from it. He would come into this from the back, creep cautiously through it, taking care that no twigs cracked, and then, drawing himself on his stomach to the edge, peer down upon the scene below him. People were always doing that sort of thing in books, and he had been filled with a hopeless envy of them; well, now he was actually going to do it himself. What fun!

And then, when he had got back unobserved to the house and reported to Antony, they were going to explore the secret passage! Again, what fun! Unfortunately there seemed to be no chance of buried treasure, but there might be buried clues. Even if you found nothing, you couldn't get away from the fact that a secret passage is a secret passage, and anything might happen in it. But even that wasn't the end of this exciting day. They were going to watch the pond that night; they were going to watch Cayley under the moonlight, watch him as he threw into the silence of the pond—what? The revolver? Well, anyhow, they were going to watch him. What fun!

To Antony, who was older and who realized into

what deep waters they were getting, it did not seem fun. But it was amazingly interesting. He saw so much, and yet somehow it was all out of focus. It was like looking at an opal, and discovering with every movement of it some new colour, some new gleam of light reflected, and yet never really seeing the opal as a whole. He was too near it, or too far away; he strained his eyes and he relaxed his eyes; it was no good. His brain could not get hold of it.

But there were moments when he almost had it . . . and then turned away from it. He had seen more of life than Bill, but he had never seen murder before, and this which was in his mind now, and to which he was afraid to listen, was not just the hot-blooded killing which any man may come to if he lose control. It was something much more horrible. Too horrible to be true. Then let him look again for the truth. He looked again—but it was all out of focus.

"I will *not* look again," he said aloud, as he began to walk towards the house. "Not yet, anyway." He would go on collecting facts and impressions. Perhaps the one fact would come along by itself which would make everything clear.

CHAPTER XIV

MR. BEVERLEY QUALIFIES FOR THE STAGE

Bill had come back, and had reported, rather breathless, that Cayley was still at the pond.

"But I don't think they're getting up much except mud," he said. "I ran most of the way back so as to give us as much time as possible."

Antony nodded.

"Well, come along, then," he said. "The sooner, the quicker."

They stood in front of the row of sermons. Antony took down the Reverend Theodore Ussher's famous volume, and felt for the spring. Bill pulled. The shelves swung open toward them.

"By Jove!" said Bill, "it *is* a narrow way."

There was an opening about a yard square in front of them, which had something the look of a brick fireplace, a fireplace raised about two feet from the ground. But, save for one row of bricks in front, the floor of it was emptiness. Antony took a torch from his pocket and flashed it down into the blackness.

"Look," he whispered to the eager Bill. "The steps begin down there. Six feet down."

He flashed his torch up again. There was a handhold of iron, a sort of large iron staple, in the bricks in front of them.

"You swung off from there," said Bill. "At least,

I suppose you do. I wonder how Ruth Norris liked doing it."

"Cayley helped her, I should think. . . . It's funny."

"Shall I go first?" asked Bill, obviously longing to do so.

Antony shook his head with a smile.

"I think I will, if you don't mind very much, Bill. Just in case."

"In case of what?"

"Well—in case."

Bill had to be content with that, but he was too much excited to wonder what Antony meant.

"Righto," he said. "Go on."

"Well, we'll just make sure we can get back again, first. It really wouldn't be fair on the inspector if we got stuck down here for the rest of our lives. He's got enough to do trying to find Mark, but if he has to find you and me as well——"

"We can always get out at the other end."

"Well, we're not certain yet. I think I'd better just go down and back. I promise faithfully not to explore."

"Right you are."

Antony sat down on the ledge of bricks, swung his feet over, and sat there for a moment, his legs dangling. He flashed his torch into the darkness again, so as to make sure where the steps began; then returned it to his pocket, seized the staple in front of him and swung himself down. His feet touched the steps beneath him, and he let go.

"Is it all right?" said Bill anxiously.

"All right. I'll just go down to the bottom of the steps and back. Stay there."

The light shone down by his feet. His head began to disappear. For a little while Bill, craning down the opening, could still see faint splashes of light, and could hear slow uncertain footsteps; for a little longer he could fancy that he saw and heard them; then he was alone. . . .

Well, not quite alone. There was a sudden voice in the hall outside.

"Good Lord!" said Bill, turning round with a start. "Cayley!"

If he was not so quick in thought as Antony, he was quick enough in action. Thought was not demanded now. To close the secret door safely but noiselessly, to make sure that the books were in the right places, to move away to another row of shelves so as to be discovered deep in "Badminton" or "Baedeker" or whomever the kind gods should send to his aid—the difficulty was not to decide what to do, but to do all this in five seconds rather than in six.

"Ah, there you are," said Cayley from the doorway.

"Hallo!" said Bill, in surprise, looking up from the fourth volume of "The Life and Works of Samuel Taylor Coleridge." "Have they finished?"

"Finished what?"

"The pond," said Bill, wondering why he was reading Coleridge on such a fine afternoon. Desperately he tried to think of a good reason . . . verifying a quotation—an argument with Antony—that would do. But *what* quotation?

"Oh, no. They're still at it. Where's Gillingham?"

"The Ancient Mariner"—water, water, everywhere —or was that something else? And where was Gillingham? Water, water everywhere——

"Tony? Oh, he's about somewhere. We're just going down to the village. They aren't finding anything at the pond, are they?"

"No. But they like doing it. Something off their minds when they can say they've done it."

Bill, deep in his book, looked up and said "Yes," and went back to it again. He was just getting to the place.

"What's the book?" said Cayley, coming up to him. Out of the corner of his eye he glanced at the shelf of sermons as he came. Bill saw that glance and wondered. Was there anything there to give away the secret?

"I was just looking up a quotation," he drawled. "Tony and I had a bet about it. You know that thing about—er—water, water everywhere, and—er—not a drop to drink." (But what on earth, he wondered to himself, were they betting about?)

" 'Nor any drop to drink,' to be accurate."

Bill looked at him in surprise. Then a happy smile came on his face.

"Quite sure?" he said.

"Of course."

"Then you've saved me a lot of trouble. That's what the bet was about." He closed the book with a slam, put it back in its shelf, and began to feel for his pipe and tobacco. "I was a fool to bet with Tony," he added. "He always knows that sort of thing."

So far, so good. But here was Cayley still in the library, and there was Antony, all unsuspecting, in the passage. When Antony came back he would not be surprised to find the door closed, because the whole object of his going had been to see if he could open the door easily from the inside. At any moment, then, the bookshelf might swing back and show Antony's head in the gap. A nice surprise for Cayley!

"Come with us?" he said casually, as he struck a match. He pulled vigorously at the flame as he waited for the answer, hoping to hide his anxiety, for if Cayley assented, he was done.

"I've got to go into Stanton."

Bill blew out a great cloud of smoke with an expiration which covered also a heartfelt sigh of relief.

"Oh, a pity. You're driving, I suppose?"

"Yes. The car will be here directly. There's a letter I must write first." He sat down at a writing table, and took out a sheet of notepaper.

He was facing the secret door; if it opened he would see it. And any moment now it might open.

Bill dropped into a chair and thought. Antony must be warned. Obviously. But how? How did one signal to anybody? By code. Morse code. Did Antony know it? Did Bill know it himself, if it came to that? He had picked up a bit in the Army—not enough to send a message, of course. But a message was impossible, anyhow; Cayley would hear him tapping it out. It wouldn't do to send more than a single letter. What letters did he know? And what letter would convey anything to Antony? . . . He pulled at his pipe, his eyes wandering from Cayley at his desk to the Reverend Theodore Ussher in his shelf. What letter?

C for Cayley. Would Antony understand? Probably not, but it was just worth trying. What was C? Long, short, long, short. Umpty-iddy-umpty-iddy. Was that right? C—yes, that was C. He was sure of that. C. Umpty-iddy-umpty-iddy.

Hands in pockets, he got up and wandered across the room, humming vaguely to himself, the picture of a man waiting for another man (as it might be his friend Gillingham) to come in and take him away for a walk or something. He wandered across to the books at the back of Cayley, and began to tap absent-mindedly on the shelves, as he looked at the titles. Umpty-iddy-umpty-iddy. Not that it was much like that at first; he couldn't get the rhythm of it. . . .

Umpt-y-iddy-*umpt*-y-iddy. That was better. He was back at Samuel Taylor Coleridge now. Antony would begin to hear him soon. *Umpt*-y-iddy-*umpt*-y-iddy; just the aimless tapping of a man who is wondering what book he will take out with him to read on the lawn. Would Antony hear? One always heard the man in the next flat knocking out his pipe. Would Antony understand? *Umpt*-y-iddy-*umpt*-y-iddy. C. for Cayley, Antony. Cayley's here. For God's sake, wait.

"Good Lord! Sermons!" said Bill, with a loud laugh. (*Umpt*-y-iddy-*umpt*-y-iddy.) "Ever read 'em, Cayley?"

"What?" Cayley looked up suddenly. Bill's back moved slowly along, his fingers beating a tattoo on the shelves as he walked.

"Er—no," said Cayley, with a little laugh. An awkward, uncomfortable little laugh, it seemed to Bill.

"Nor do I." He was past the sermons now—past the secret door—but still tapping in the same aimless way.

"Oh, for God's sake sit down," burst out Cayley. "Or go outside if you want to walk about."

Bill turned round in astonishment.

"Hallo, what's the matter?"

Cayley was slightly ashamed of his outburst.

"Sorry, Bill," he apologized. "My nerves are on edge. Your constant tapping and fidgeting about——"

"Tapping?" said Bill with an air of complete surprise.

"Tapping on the shelves, and humming. Sorry. It got on my nerves."

"My dear old chap, I'm awfully sorry. I'll go out in the hall."

"It's all right," said Cayley, and went on with his letter.

Bill sat down in his chair again. Had Antony understood? Well, anyhow, there was nothing to do now but wait for Cayley to go. "And if you ask *me*," said Bill to himself, much pleased, "I ought to be on the stage. That's where I ought to be. The complete actor."

A minute, two minutes, three minutes . . . five minutes. It was safe now. Antony had guessed.

"Is the car there?" asked Cayley, as he sealed up his letter.

Bill strolled into the hall, called back "Yes," and went out to talk to the chauffeur. Cayley joined him, and they stood there for a moment.

"Hallo," said a pleasant voice behind them. They turned round and saw Antony.

"Sorry to keep you waiting, Bill."

With a tremendous effort Bill restrained his feelings, and said casually enough that it was all right.

"Well, I must be off," said Cayley. "You're going down to the village?"

"That's the idea."

"I wonder if you'd take this letter to Jallands for me?"

"Of course."

"Thanks very much. Well, I shall see you later." He nodded and got into the car.

As soon as they were alone Bill turned eagerly to his friend.

"Well?" he said excitedly.

"Come into the library."

They went in, and Tony sank down into a chair.

"You must give me a moment," he panted. "I've been running."

"Running?"

"Well, of course. How do you think I got back here?"

"You don't mean you went out at the other end?"

Antony nodded.

"I say, did you hear me tapping?"

"I did, indeed. Bill, you're a genius."

Bill blushed.

"I knew you'd understand," he said. "You guessed that I meant Cayley?"

"I did. It was the least I could do after you had been so brilliant. You must have had rather an exciting time."

"Exciting? Good lord, I should think it was."

"Tell me about it."

As modestly as possible, Mr. Beverley explained his qualifications for life on the stage.

"Good man," said Antony at the end of it. "You are the most perfect Watson that ever lived. Bill, my lad," he went on dramatically, rising and taking Bill's hand in both of his, "there is nothing that you and I could not accomplish together, if we gave our minds to it."

"Silly old ass."

"That's what you always say when I'm being serious. Well, anyway, thanks awfully. You really saved us this time."

"Were you coming back?"

"Yes. At least I think I was. I was just wondering when I heard you tapping. The fact of the door being shut was rather surprising. Of course the whole idea was to see if it could be opened easily from the other side, but I felt somehow that you wouldn't shut it until the last possible moment—until you saw me coming back. Well, then I heard the taps, and I knew it must mean something, so I sat tight. Then when C began to come along I said, 'Cayley, b'Jove'—bright, aren't I?—and I simply hared to the other end of the passage for all I was worth. And hared back again. Because I thought you might be getting rather involved in explanations—about where I was, and so on."

"You didn't see Mark, then?"

"No. Nor his—— No, I didn't see anything."

"Nor what?"

Antony was silent for a moment.

"I didn't see anything, Bill. Or rather, I did see something; I saw a door in the wall, a cupboard. And it's locked. So if there's anything we want to find, that's where it is."

"Could Mark be hiding there?"

"I called through the keyhole—in a whisper—'Mark, are you there?'—he would have thought it was Cayley. There was no answer."

"Well, let's go down and try again. We might be able to get the door open."

Antony shook his head.

"Aren't I going at all?" said Bill in great disappointment.

When Antony spoke, it was to ask another question:

"Can Cayley drive a car?"

"Yes, of course. Why?"

"Then he might easily drop the chauffeur at his lodge and go off to Stanton, or wherever he wanted to, on his own?"

"I suppose so—if he wanted to."

"Yes." Antony got up. "Well, look here, as we said we were going into the village, and as we promised to leave that letter, I almost think we'd better do it."

"Oh! . . . Oh, very well."

"Jallands. What were you telling me about that? Oh, yes; the Widow Norbury."

"That's right. Cayley used to be rather keen on the daughter. The letter's for her."

"Yes; well, let's take it. Just to be on the safe side."

"Am I going to be done out of that secret passage altogether?" asked Bill fretfully.

"There's nothing to see, really, I promise you."

"You're very mysterious. What's upset you? You did see something down there, I'm certain of it."

"I did, and I've told you about it."

"No, you haven't. You only told me about the door in the wall."

"That's it, Bill. And it's locked. And I'm frightened of what's behind it."

"But then we shall never know what's there if we aren't going to look."

"We shall know to-night," said Antony, taking Bill's arm and leading him to the hall, "when we watch our dear friend Cayley dropping it into the pond."

CHAPTER XV

MRS. NORBURY CONFIDES IN DEAR MR. GILLINGHAM

They left the road, and took the path across the fields which sloped gently downwards towards Jallands. Antony was silent, and since it is difficult to keep up a conversation with a silent man for any length of time, Bill had dropped into silence too. Or rather, he hummed to himself, hit at thistles in the grass with his stick and made uncomfortable noises with his pipe. But he noticed that his companion kept looking back over his shoulder, almost as if he wanted to remember for a future occasion the way by which they were coming. Yet there was no difficulty about it, for they remained all the time in view of the road, and the belt of trees above the long park wall which bordered its further side stood out clearly against the sky.

Antony, who had just looked round again, turned back with a smile.

"What's the joke?" said Bill, glad of the more social atmosphere.

"Cayley. Didn't you see?"

"See what?"

"The car. Going past on the road there."

"So *that's* what you were looking for. You've got jolly good eyes, my boy, if you recognize the car at this distance after only seeing it twice."

"Well, I *have* got jolly good eyes."

"I thought he was going to Stanton."

"He hoped you'd think so—obviously."

"Then where *is* he going?"

"The library, probably. To consult our friend Ussher. After making quite sure that his friends Beverley and Gillingham really *were* going to Jallands, as they said."

Bill stopped suddenly in the middle of the path.

"I say, do you think so?"

Antony shrugged his shoulders.

"I shouldn't be surprised. We must be devilishly inconvenient for him, hanging about the house. Any moment he can get, when we're definitely somewhere else, must be very useful to him."

"Useful for what?"

"Well, useful for his nerves, if for nothing else. We know he's mixed up in this business; we know he's hiding a secret or two. Even if he doesn't suspect that we're on his tracks, he must feel that at any moment we might stumble on something."

Bill gave a grunt of assent, and they went slowly on again.

"What about to-night?" he said after a lengthy blow at his pipe.

"Try a piece of grass," said Antony, offering it to him.

Bill pushed it through the mouthpiece, blew again, said, "That's better," and returned the pipe to his pocket.

"How are we going to get out without Cayley knowing?"

"Well, that wants thinking over. It's going to be difficult. I wish we were sleeping at the inn. . . . Is this Miss Norbury, by any chance?"

Bill looked up quickly. They were close to Jallands now, an old thatched farmhouse which, after centuries of sleep, had woken up to a new world, and had forthwith sprouted wings; wings, however, of so discreet a growth that they had not brought with them any obvious change of character, and Jallands even with a bathroom was still Jallands. To the outward view, at any rate. Inside, it was more clearly Mrs. Norbury's.

"Yes—Angela Norbury," murmured Bill. "Not bad-looking, is she?"

The girl who stood by the little white gate of Jallands was something more than "not bad-looking," but in this matter Bill was keeping his superlatives for another. In Bill's eyes she must be judged, and condemned, by all that distinguished her from Betty Calladine. To Antony, unhampered by these standards of comparison, she seemed, quite simply, beautiful.

"Cayley asked us to bring a letter along," explained Bill, when the necessary handshakings and introductions were over. "Here you are."

"You will tell him, won't you, how dreadfully sorry I am about—about what has happened? It seems so hopeless to say anything; so hopeless even to believe it. If it is true what we've heard."

Bill repeated the outline of the events of yesterday.

"Yes. . . . And Mr. Ablett hasn't been found yet?"

"No."

She shook her head in distress. "It still seems to have happened to somebody else; somebody we didn't know at all." Then, with a sudden grave smile which included both of them, "But you must come and have some tea."

"It's awfully decent of you," said Bill awkwardly, "but we—er——"

"You will, won't you?" she said to Antony.

"Thank you very much."

Mrs. Norbury was delighted to see them as she always was to see any man in her house who came up to the necessary standard of eligibility. When her life-work was completed, and summed up in those beautiful words: "A marriage has been arranged, and will shortly take place, between Angela, daughter of the late John Norbury . . ." then she would utter a grateful *Nunc dimittis* and depart in peace—to a better world, if Heaven insisted, but preferably to her new son-in-law's more dignified establishment. For there was no doubt that eligibility meant not only eligibility as a husband.

But it was not as "eligibles" that the visitors from the Red House were received with such eagerness to-day, and even if her special smile for "possibles" was there, it was instinctive rather than reasoned. All that she wanted at this moment was news—news of Mark. For she was bringing it off at last; and, if the engagement columns of the "Morning Post" were preceded, as in the case of its obituary columns, by a premonitory bulletin, the announcement of yesterday would have cried triumphantly to the world, or to such part of the world as mattered: "A marriage has very nearly been arranged (by Mrs. Norbury), and will certainly take place, between Angela, only daughter of the late John Norbury, and Mark Ablett of the Red House." And, coming across it on his way to the sporting page, Bill would have been surprised. For he had thought that, if anybody, it was Cayley.

To the girl it was neither. She was often amused by her mother's ways; sometimes ashamed of them; sometimes distressed by them. The Mark Ablett affair had seemed to her particularly distressing, for Mark was so obviously in league with her mother against her. Other suitors, upon whom her mother had smiled, had been embarrassed by that championship; Mark appeared to depend on it as much as on his own attractions, great though he thought these to be. They went a-wooing together. It was a pleasure to turn to Cayley, that hopeless ineligible.

But alas! Cayley had misunderstood her. She could not imagine Cayley in love—until she saw it, and tried, too late, to stop it. That was four days ago. She had not seen him since, and now here was this letter. She dreaded opening it. It was a relief to feel that at least she had an excuse for not doing so while her guests were in the house.

Mrs. Norbury recognized at once that Antony was likely to be the more sympathetic listener; and when tea was over, and Bill and Angela had been dispatched to the garden with the promptness and efficiency of the expert, dear Mr. Gillingham found himself on the sofa beside her, listening to many things which were of even greater interest to him than she could possibly have hoped.

"It is terrible, terrible," she said. "And to suggest that dear Mr. Ablett——"

Antony made suitable noises.

"You've seen Mr. Ablett for yourself. A kinder, more warmhearted man——"

Antony explained that he had not seen Mr. Ablett.

"Of course, yes, I was forgetting. But, believe me, Mr. Gillingham, you can trust a woman's intuition in these matters."

Antony said that he was sure of this.

"Think of my feelings as a mother."

Antony was thinking of Miss Norbury's feelings

as a daughter, and wondering if she guessed that her affairs were now being discussed with a stranger. Yet what could he do? What, indeed, did he want to do except listen, in the hope of learning? Mark engaged, or about to be engaged! Had that any bearing on the events of yesterday? What, for instance, would Mrs. Norbury have thought of brother Robert, that family skeleton? Was this another reason for wanting brother Robert out of the way?

"I never liked him, never!"

"Never liked——?" said Antony, bewildered.

"That cousin of his—Mr. Cayley."

"Oh!"

"I ask you, Mr. Gillingham, am I the sort of woman to trust my little girl to a man who would go about shooting his only brother?"

"I'm sure you wouldn't, Mrs. Norbury."

"If there has been any shooting done, it has been done by somebody else.

Antony looked at her inquiringly.

"I never liked him," said Mrs. Norbury firmly. "Never."

However, thought Antony to himself, that didn't quite prove that Cayley was a murderer.

"How did Miss Norbury get on with him?" he asked cautiously.

"There was *nothing* in that at all," said Miss Norbury's mother emphatically. "*Nothing.* I would say so to anybody."

"Oh, I beg your pardon. I never meant——"

"Nothing. I can say that for dear Angela with perfect confidence. Whether *he* made advances——" She broke off with a shrug of her plump shoulders.

Antony waited eagerly.

"Naturally they met. Possibly he might have—I don't know. But my duty as a mother was clear, Mr. Gillingham."

Mr. Gillingham made an encouraging noise.

"I told him quite frankly that—how shall I put it?—that he was trespassing. Tactfully, of *course*. But frankly."

"You mean," said Antony, trying to speak calmly, "that you told him that—er—Mr. Ablett and your daughter——?"

Mrs. Norbury nodded several times.

"Exactly, Mr. Gillingham. I had my duty as a mother."

"I am sure, Mrs. Norbury, that nothing would keep you from doing your duty. But it must have been disagreeable. Particularly if you weren't quite sure—"

"He was attracted, Mr. Gillingham. Obviously attracted."

"Who would not be?" said Antony, with a charming smile. "It must have been something of a shock to him to——"

"It was just that which made me so glad that I had spoken. I saw at once that I had not spoken a moment too soon."

"There must have been a certain awkwardness about the next meeting," suggested Antony.

"Naturally, he has not been here since. No doubt they would have been bound to meet up at the Red House sooner or later."

"Oh, this was only quite lately?"

"Last week, Mr. Gillingham. I spoke just in time."

"Ah!" said Antony, under his breath. He had been waiting for it.

He would have liked now to have gone away, so that he might have thought over the new situation by himself; or, perhaps preferably, to have changed partners for a little while with Bill. Miss Norbury would hardly be ready to confide in a stranger with the readiness of a mother, but he might have learnt something by listening to her. For which of them had she the greater feeling—Cayley or Mark? Was she really prepared to marry Mark? Did she love him—or the other—or neither? Mrs. Norbury was only a trustworthy witness in regard to her own actions and thoughts; he had learnt all that was necessary of those, and only the daughter now had anything left to tell him. But Mrs. Norbury was still talking.

"Girls are so foolish, Mr. Gillingham," she was saying. "It is fortunate that they have mothers to guide them. It was so obvious to me from the beginning that dear Mr. Ablett was just the husband for my little girl. You never knew him?"

Antony said again that he had not seen Mr. Ablett.

"Such a gentleman. So nice-looking, in his artistic way. A regular Velazquez—I should say Van Dyck. Angela would have it that she could never marry a man with a beard. As if *that* mattered, when——" She broke off, and Antony finished her sentence for her.

"The Red House is certainly charming," he said.

"Charming. Quite charming. And it is not as if Mr. Ablett's appearance were in any way undistinguished. Quite the contrary. I'm sure you agree with me?"

Antony said that he had never had the pleasure of seeing Mr. Ablett.

"Yes. And quite the centre of the literary and artistic world. So desirable in every way."

She gave a deep sigh, and communed with herself for a little. Antony was about to snatch the opportunity of leaving, when Mrs. Norbury began again.

"And then there's this scapegrace brother of his. He was perfectly frank with me, Mr. Gillingham. He would be. He told me of this brother, and I told him that I was quite certain it would make no difference to my daughter's feelings for him. . . . After all, the brother was in Australia."

"When was this? Yesterday?" Antony felt that, if Mark had only mentioned it after his brother's announcement of a personal call at the Red House, this perfect frankness had a good deal of wisdom behind it.

"It couldn't have been yesterday, Mr. Gillingham. Yesterday——" she shuddered, and shook her head.

"I thought perhaps he had been down here in the morning."

"Oh, no! There is such a thing, Mr. Gillingham, as being too devoted a lover. Not in the morning, no. We both agreed that dear Angela— Oh, no. No; the day before yesterday, when he happened to drop in about tea-time."

It occurred to Antony that Mrs. Norbury had come a long way from her opening statement that Mark and Miss Norbury were practically engaged. She was now admitting that dear Angela was not to be rushed, that dear Angela had, indeed, no heart for the match at all.

"The day before yesterday. As it happened, dear Angela was out. Not that it mattered. He was driving to Middleston. He hardly had time for a cup of tea, so that even if she had been in——"

Antony nodded absently. This was something new. Why did Mark go to Middleston the day before yesterday? But, after all, why shouldn't he? A hundred reasons unconnected with the death of Robert might have taken him there.

He got up to go. He wanted to be alone—alone, at least, with Bill. Mrs. Norbury had given him many things to think over, but the greater outstanding fact which had emerged was this: that Cayley had reason to hate Mark. Mrs. Norbury had given him that reason. To hate? Well, to be jealous, anyhow. But that was enough.

"You see," he said to Bill, as they walked back, "we know that Cayley is perjuring himself and risking himself over this business, and that must be for one of two reasons. Either to save Mark or to endanger him. That is to say, he is either whole-heartedly for him or whole-heartedly against him. Well, now we know that he is against him, definitely against him."

"But, I say, you know," protested Bill, "one doesn't necessarily try to ruin one's rival in love."

"Doesn't one?" said Antony, turning to him with a smile.

Bill blushed.

"Well, of course, one never knows, but I mean——"

"You mightn't try to ruin him, Bill, but you wouldn't perjure yourself in order to get him out of a trouble of his own making."

"Lord! no."

"So that of the two alternatives the other is the more likely."

They had come to the gate into the last field which divided them from the road, and having gone through it, they turned round and leant against it, resting for a moment, and looking down at the house which they had left.

"Jolly little place, isn't it?" said Bill.

"Very. But rather mysterious."

"In what way?"

"Well, where's the front door?"

"The front door? Why, you've just come out of it."

"But isn't there a drive, or a road or anything?" Bill laughed.

"No; that's the beauty of it to some people. And that's why it's so cheap, and why the Norburys can afford it, I expect. They're not too well off."

"But what about luggage and tradesmen and that kind of thing?"

"Oh, there's a cart-track, but motor-cars can't come any nearer than the road"—he turned round and pointed—"up there. So the week-end millionaire people don't take it. At least, they'd have to build a road and a garage and all the rest of it, if they did."

"I see," said Antony carelessly, and they turned round and continued their walk up to the road. But later on he remembered this casual conversation at the gate, and saw the importance of it.

CHAPTER XVI

GETTING READY FOR THE NIGHT

What was it which Cayley was going to hide in that pond that night? Antony thought that he knew now. It was Mark's body.

From the beginning he had seen this answer coming and had drawn back from it. For, if Mark had been killed, it seemed such a cold-blooded killing. Was Cayley equal to it? Bill would have said "No," but that was because he had had breakfast with Cayley, and lunch with him, and dinner with him; had ragged him and played games with him. Bill would have said "No," because Bill wouldn't have killed anybody in cold blood himself, and because he took it for granted that other people behaved pretty much as he did. But Antony had no such illusions. Murders were done; murder had actually been done here, for there was Robert's dead body. Why not another murder?

Had Mark been in the office at all that afternoon? The only evidence (other than Cayley's, which obviously did not count) was Elsie's. Elsie was quite certain that she had heard his voice. But then Bill had said that it was a very characteristic voice—an easy voice, therefore, to imitate. If Bill could imitate it so successfully, why not Cayley?

But perhaps it had not been such a cold-blooded

killing, after all. Suppose Cayley had had a quarrel with his cousin that afternoon over the girl whom they were both wooing. Suppose Cayley had killed Mark, either purposely, in sudden passion, or accidentally, meaning only to knock him down. Suppose that this had happened in the passage, say about two o'clock, either because Cayley had deliberately led him there, or because Mark had casually suggested a visit to it. (One could imagine Mark continually gloating over that secret passage.) Suppose Cayley there, with the body at his feet, feeling already the rope round his neck; his mind darting this way and that in frantic search for a way of escape; and suppose that suddenly and irrelevantly he remembers that Robert is coming to the house at three o'clock that afternoon—automatically he looks at his watch —in half an hour's time. . . .

In half an hour's time. He must think of something quickly, quickly. Shall he bury the body in the passage and let it be thought that Mark ran away, frightened at the mere thought of his brother's arrival? But there was the evidence of the breakfast table. Mark had seemed annoyed at this resurrection of the black sheep, but certainly not frightened. No, that was much too thin a story. But suppose Mark had actually seen his brother and had a quarrel with him; suppose it could be made to look as if Robert had killed Mark——

Antony pictured to himself Cayley in the passage, standing over the dead body of his cousin, and working it out. How could Robert be made to seem the murderer, if Robert were alive to deny it? But suppose Robert were dead, too?

He looks at his watch again. (Only twenty-five minutes now.) Suppose Robert were dead, too? Robert

dead in the office, and Mark dead in the passage—
how does that help? Madness! But if the bodies were
brought together somehow . . . and Robert's death
looked like suicide? . . . Was it possible?

Madness again. Too difficult. (Only twenty minutes now.) Too difficult to arrange in twenty minutes. Can't arrange a suicide. Too difficult. . . . Only
nineteen minutes. . . .

And then the sudden inspiration! Robert dead in
the office, Mark's body hidden in the passage—impossible to make Robert seem the murderer, but how
easy to make Mark! Robert dead and Mark missing;
why, it jumped to the eye at once. Mark had killed
Robert—accidentally; yes, that would be more likely—
and then had run away. Sudden panic. . . . (He looks
at his watch again. Fifteen minutes, but plenty of
time now. The thing arranges itself.)

Was that the solution, Antony wondered. It seemed
to fit in with the facts as they knew them; but then, so
did that other theory which he had suggested to Bill
in the morning.

"Which one?" said Bill.

They had come back from Jallands through the
park and were sitting in the copse above the pond,
from which the inspector and his fishermen had now
withdrawn. Bill had listened with open mouth to
Antony's theory, and save for an occasional "By Jove!"
had listened in silence. "Smart man, Cayley," had been
his only comment at the end.

"Which other theory?"

"That Mark had killed Robert accidentally and
had gone to Cayley for help, and that Cayley, having
hidden him in the passage, locked the office door from
the outside and hammered on it."

"Yes, but you were so dashed mysterious about

that. I asked you what the point of it was, and you wouldn't say anything." He thought for a little, and then went on. "I suppose you meant that Cayley deliberately betrayed Mark, and tried to make him look like a murderer?"

"I wanted to warn you that we should probably find Mark in the passage, alive or dead."

"And now you don't think so?"

"Now I think that his dead body is there."

"Meaning that Cayley went down and killed him afterwards—after you had come, after the police had come?"

"Well, that's what I shrink from, Bill. It's so horribly cold-blooded. Cayley may be capable of it, but I hate to think of it."

"But, dash it all, your other way is cold-blooded enough. According to you, he goes up to the office and deliberately shoots a man with whom he has no quarrel, whom he hasn't seen for fifteen years!"

"Yes, but to save his own neck. That makes a difference. My theory is that he quarrelled violently with Mark over the girl, and killed him in sudden passion. Anything that happened after that would be self-defence. I don't mean that I excuse it, but that I understand it. And I think that Mark's dead body is in the passage now, and has been there since, say, half-past two yesterday afternoon. And to-night Cayley is going to hide it in the pond."

Bill pulled at the moss on the ground beside him, threw away a handful or two, and said slowly, "You may be right, but it's all guess-work, you know."

Antony laughed.

"Good Lord, of course it is," he said. "And tonight we shall know if it's a good guess or a bad one."

Bill brightened up suddenly.

"To-night," he said. "I say, to-night's going to be rather fun. How do we work it?"

Antony was silent for a little.

"Of course," he said at last, "we ought to inform the police, so that they can come here and watch the pond to-night."

"Of course," grinned Bill.

"But I think that perhaps it is a little early to put our theories before them."

"I think perhaps it is," said Bill solemnly.

Antony looked up at him with a sudden smile.

"Bill, you old bounder."

"Well, dash it, it's *our* show. I don't see why we shouldn't get our little bit of fun out of it."

"Neither do I. All right, then, we'll do without the police to-night."

"We shall miss them," said Bill sadly, "but 'tis better so."

There were two problems in front of them: first, the problem of getting out of the house without being discovered by Cayley, and secondly, the problem of recovering whatever it was which Cayley dropped into the pond that night.

"Let's look at it from Cayley's point of view," said Antony. "He may not know that we're on his track, but he can't help being suspicious of us. He's bound to be suspicious of everybody in the house, and more particularly of us, because we're presumably more intelligent than the others."

He stopped for a moment to light his pipe, and Bill took the opportunity of looking more intelligent than Mrs. Stevens.

"Now, he has got something to hide to-night, and he's going to take good care that we aren't watching him. Well, what will he do?"

"See that we are asleep first, before he starts out."

"Yes. Come and tuck us up, and see that we're nice and comfortable."

"Yes, that's awkward," said Bill. "But we could lock our doors, and then he wouldn't know that we weren't there."

"Have you ever locked your door?"

"Never."

"No. And you can bet that Cayley knows that. Anyway, he'd bang on it, and you wouldn't answer, and then what would he think?"

Bill was silent; crushed.

"Then I don't see how we're going to do it," he said, after deep thought. "He'll obviously come to us just before he starts out, and that doesn't give us time to get to the pond in front of him."

"Let's put ourselves in his place," said Antony, puffing slowly at his pipe. "He's got the body, or whatever it is, in the passage. He won't come up the stairs, carrying it in his arms, and look in at our doors to see if we're awake. He'll have to make sure about us first, and then go down for the body afterwards. So that gives us a little time."

"Y—yes," said Bill thoughtfully. "We might just do it, but it'll be a bit of a rush."

"But wait. When he's gone down to the passage and got the body, what will he do next?"

"Come out again," said Bill helpfully.

"Yes; but which end?"

Bill sat up with a start.

"By Jove, you mean that he will go out at the far end by the bowling-green?"

"Don't you think so? Just imagine him walking across the lawn in full view of the house, at midnight, with a body in his arms. Think of the awful feeling he would have in the back of the neck, wondering if anybody, any restless sleeper, had chosen just that moment to wander to the window and look out into the night. There's still plenty of moonlight, Bill. Is he going to walk across the park in the moonlight, with all those windows staring at him? Not if he can help it. But he can get out by the bowling green, and then come to the pond without ever being in sight of the house at all."

"You're right. And that will just about give us time. Good. Now, what's the next thing?"

"The next thing is to mark the exact place in the pond where he drops—whatever he drops."

"So that we can fish it out again."

"If we can see what it is, we shan't want to. The police can have a go at it to-morrow. But if it's something we can't identify from a distance, then we must try and get it out. To see whether it's worth telling the police about."

"Y—yes," said Bill, wrinkling his forehead. "Of course, the trouble with water is that one bit of it looks pretty much like the next bit. I don't know if that had occurred to you."

"It had," smlied Antony. "Let's come and have a look at it."

They walked to the edge of the copse, and lay down there in silence, looking at the pond beneath them.

"See anything?" said Antony at last.

"What?"

"The fence on the other side."

"What about it?"

"Well, it's rather useful, that's all."

"Said Sherlock Holmes enigmatically," added Bill. "A moment later, his friend Watson had hurled him into the pond."

Antony laughed.

"I love being Sherlocky," he said. "It's very unfair of you not to play up to me."

"Why is that fence useful, my dear Holmes?" said Bill obediently.

"Because you can take a bearing on it. You see——"

"Yes, you needn't stop to explain to me what a bearing is."

"I wasn't going to. But you're lying here"—he looked up—"underneath this pine-tree. Cayley comes out in the old boat and drops his parcel in. You take a line from here on to the boat, and mark it off on the fence there. Say it's the fifth post from the end. Well, then I take a line from *my* tree—we'll find one for me directly—and it comes on to the twentieth post, say. And where the two lines meet, there shall the eagles be gathered together. Q.E.D. And there, I almost forgot to remark, will the taller eagle, Beverley by name, do his famous diving act. As performed nightly at the Hippodrome."

Bill looked at him uneasily.

"I say, really? It's beastly dirty water, you know."

"I'm afraid so, Bill. So it is written in the book of Jasher."

"Of course I knew that one of us would have to, but I hoped—oh, well, it's a warm night."

"Just the night for a bathe," agreed Antony, getting up. "Well now, let's have a look for my tree."

They walked down to the margin of the pond and then looked back. Bill's tree stood up and took the evening, tall and unmistakable, fifty feet nearer to heaven than its neighbours. But it had its fellow at the other end of the copse, not quite so tall, perhaps, but equally conspicuous.

"That's where I shall be," said Antony, pointing to it. "Now, for the Lord's sake, count your posts accurately."

"Thanks very much, but I shall do it for my own sake," said Bill with feeling. "I don't want to spend the whole night diving."

"Fix on the post in a straight line with you and the splash, and then count backwards to the beginning of the fence."

"Right, old boy. Leave it to me. I can do this on my head."

"Well, that's how you will have to do the last part of it," said Antony with a smile.

He looked at his watch. It was nearly time to change for dinner. They started to walk back to the house together.

"There's one thing which worries me rather," said Antony. "Where does Cayley sleep?"

"Next door to me. Why?"

"Well, it's just possible that he might have another look at you after he's come back from the pond. I don't think he'd bother about it in the ordinary way, but if he is actually passing your door, I think he might glance in."

"I shan't be there. I shall be at the bottom of the pond, sucking up mud."

"Yes. . . . Do you think you could leave something in your bed that looked vaguely like you in the dark? A bolster with a pyjama-coat round it, and one arm outside the blanket, and a pair of socks or something for the head. You know the kind of thing. I think it would please him to feel that you were still sleeping peacefully."

Bill chuckled to himself.

"Rather. I'm awfully good at that. I'll make him up something really good. But what about you?"

"I'm at the other end of the house; he's hardly likely to bother about me a second time. And I shall be so very fast asleep at his first visit. Still, I may as well—to be on the safe side."

They went into the house. Cayley was in the hall as they came in. He nodded, and took out his watch.

"Time to change?" he said.

"Just about," said Bill.

"You didn't forget my letter?"

"I did not. In fact, we had tea there."

"Ah!" He looked away and said carelessly, "How were they all?"

"They sent all sorts of sympathetic messages to you, and—and all that sort of thing."

"Oh, yes."

Bill waited for him to say something more, and then, as nothing was coming, he turned round, said, "Come on, Tony," and led the way upstairs.

"Got all you want?" he said at the top of the stairs.

"I think so. Come and see me before you go down."

"Righto."

Antony shut his bedroom door behind him and walked over to the window. He pushed open a casement and looked out. His bedroom was just over the door at the back of the house. The side wall of the office, which projected out into the lawn beyond the rest of the house, was on his left. He could step out on to the top of the door, and from there drop easily to the ground. Getting back would be a little more difficult. There was a convenient waterpipe which would help.

He had just finished his dressing when Bill came in.

"Final instructions?" he asked, sitting down on the bed. "By the way, how are we amusing ourselves after dinner? I mean immediately after dinner."

"Billiards?"

"Righto. Anything you like."

"Don't talk too loud," said Antony in a lower voice. "We're more or less over the hall, and Cayley may be there." He led the way to the window. "We'll go out this way to-night. Going downstairs is too risky. It's easy enough; better put on tennis-shoes."

"Right. I say, in case I don't get another chance alone with you—what do I do when Cayley comes to tuck me up?"

"It's difficult to say. Be as natural as you can. I mean, if he just knocks lightly and looks in, be asleep. Don't overdo the snoring. But if he makes a hell of a noise, you'll have to wake up and rub your eyes, and wonder what on earth he's doing in your room at all. You know the sort of thing."

"Right. And about the dummy figure. I'll make it up directly we come upstairs, and hide it under the bed."

"Yes. . . . I think we'd better go completely to bed ourselves. We shan't take a moment dressing again, and it will give him time to get safely into the passage. Then come into my room."

"Right. . . . Are you ready?"

"Yes."

They went downstairs together.

CHAPTER XVII

MR. BEVERLEY TAKES THE WATER

Cayley seemed very fond of them that night. After dinner was over, he suggested a stroll outside. They walked up and down the gravel in front of the house, saying very little to each other, until Bill could stand it no longer. For the last twenty turns he had been slowing down hopefully each time they came to the door, but the hint had always been lost on his companions, and each time another turn had been taken. But in the end he had been firm.

"What about a little billiards?" he said, shaking himself free from the others.

"Will you play?" said Antony to Cayley.

"I'll watch you," he said, and he had watched them resolutely until the game, and then another game after that, had been played.

They went into the hall and attacked the drinks.

"Well, thank heaven for bed," said Bill, putting down his glass. "Are you coming?"

"Yes," said Antony, and finished his drink. He looked at Cayley.

"I've just got one or two little things to do," said Cayley. "I shan't be long following you."

"Well, good night, then."

"Good night."

"Good night," called Bill from half-way up the stairs. "Good night, Tony."

"Good night."

Bill looked at his watch. Half-past eleven. Not much chance of anything happening for another hour. He pulled open a drawer and wondered what to wear on their expedition. Grey flannel trousers, flannel shirt, and a dark coat; perhaps a sweater, as they might be lying out in the copse for some time. And—good idea—a towel. He would want it later on, and meanwhile he could wear it round his waist. . . . Tennis-shoes. . . . There! Everything was ready. Now then for the dummy figure. . . .

He looked at his watch again before getting into bed. Twelve-fifteen. How long to wait before Cayley came up? He turned out the light, and then, standing by the door in his pyjamas, waited for his eyes to become accustomed to the new darkness. . . . He could only just make out the bed in the corner of the room. Cayley would want more light than that if he were to satisfy himself from the door that the bed was occupied. He pulled the curtains a little way back. That was about right. He could have another look later on, when he had the dummy figure in the bed. . . .

How long would it be before Cayley came up? It wasn't that he wanted his friends, Beverley and Gillingham, to be asleep before he started on his business at the pond; all that he wanted was to be sure that they were safely in their bedrooms. Cayley's business would make no noise, give no sign, to attract the most wakeful member of the household, so long as the household was really inside the house. But if he wished to reassure himself about his guests, he would have to wait until they were far enough on their way to sleep not to be disturbed by him as he came up to reassure himself. So it amounted to the same thing, really. He would wait until they were asleep . . . until they were asleep . . . asleep. . . .

With a great effort Bill regained the mastery over his wandering thoughts and came awake again. This would never do. It would be fatal if he went to sleep . . . if he went to sleep . . . to sleep. . . . And then, in an instant, he was intensely awake. Suppose Cayley never came at all!

Suppose Cayley was so unsuspicious that, as soon as they had gone upstairs, he had dived down into the passage and set about his business. Suppose, even now, he was at the pond, dropping into it that secret of his. Good heavens, what fools they had been! How could Antony have taken such a risk? Put yourself in Cayley's place, he had said. But how was it possible? They weren't Cayley. Cayley was at the pond now. They would never know what he had dropped into it.

Listen! . . . Somebody at the door. He was asleep. Quite naturally now. Breathe a little more loudly, perhaps. He was asleep. . . . The door was opening. He could feel it opening behind him. . . . Good Lord, suppose Cayley really *was* a murderer! Why, even now he might be—no, he mustn't think of that. If he thought of that, he would have to turn round. He mustn't turn round. He was asleep; just peacefully asleep. But why didn't the door shut? Where was Cayley now? Just behind him? And in his hand—no, he mustn't think of that. He was asleep. But why didn't the door shut?

The door was shutting. There was a sigh from the sleeper in the bed, a sigh of relief which escaped him involuntarily. But it had a very natural sound—a deep breath from a heavy sleeper. He added another one to it to make it seem more natural. The door was shut. . . .

Bill counted a hundred slowly and then got up. As quickly and as noiselessly as possible he dressed himself in the dark. He put the dummy figure in the bed, arranged the clothes so that just enough but not too much of it was showing, and stood by the door looking at it. For a casual glance the room was just about light enough. Then very quietly, very slowly he opened the door. All was still. There was no light from beneath the door of Cayley's room. Very quietly, very carefully he crept along the passage to Antony's room. He opened the door and went in.

Antony was still in bed. Bill walked across to wake him up, and then stopped rigid, and his heart thumped against his ribs. There was somebody else in the room.

"All right, Bill," said a whispering voice, and Antony stepped out from the curtains.

Bill gazed at him without saying anything.

"Rather good, isn't it?" said Antony, coming closer and pointing to the bed. "Come on; the sooner we get out now, the better."

He led the way out of the window, the silent Bill following him. They reached the ground safely and noiselessly, went quickly across the lawn and so over the fence, into the park. It was not until they were out of sight of the house that Bill felt it safe to speak.

"I quite thought it was you in bed," he said.

"I hoped you would. I shall be rather disappointed now if Cayley doesn't call again. It's a pity to waste it."

"He came all right just now?"

"Oh, rather. What about you?"

Bill explained his feelings picturesquely.

"There wouldn't have been much point in his killing you," said Antony prosaically. "Besides being too risky."

"Oh!" said Bill. And then, "I *had* rather hoped that it was his love for me which restrained him."

Antony laughed.

"I doubt it. . . . You didn't turn up your light when you dressed?"

"Good Lord, no. Did you want me to?"

Antony laughed again and took him by the arm.

"You're a splendid conspirator, Bill. You and I could take on anything together."

The pond was waiting for them, more solemn in the moonlight. The trees which crowned the sloping bank on the far side of it were mysteriously silent. It seemed that they had the world very much to themselves.

Almost unconsciously Antony spoke in a whisper.

"There's your tree, there's mine. As long as you don't move, there's no chance of his seeing you. After he's gone, don't come out till I do. He won't be here for a quarter of an hour or so, so don't be impatient."

"Righto," whispered Bill.

Antony gave him a nod and a smile, and they walked off to their posts.

The minutes went by slowly. To Antony, lying hidden in the undergrowth at the foot of his tree, a new problem was presenting itself. Suppose Cayley had to make more than one journey that night? He might come back to find them in the boat; one of them, indeed, in the water. And if they decided to wait in hiding, on the chance of Cayley coming back again, what was the least time they could safely allow? Perhaps it would be better to go round to the front of the house and watch for his return there, the light in his bedroom, before conducting their experiments at the pond. But then they might miss his second visit in this way, if he made a second visit. It was difficult.

His eyes were fixed on the boat as he considered these things, and suddenly, as if materialized from nowhere, Cayley was standing by the boat. In his hand was a small brown bag,

Cayley put the bag in the bottom of the boat, stepped in, and using an oar as a punt-pole, pushed slowly off. Then, very silently, he rowed towards the middle of the pond. . . .

He had stopped. The oars rested on the water. He picked up the bag from between his feet, leant over the nose of the boat, and rested it lightly on the water for a moment. Then he let go. It sank slowly. He waited there, watching; afraid, perhaps, that it might rise again.

Antony began to count. . . .

And now Cayley was back at his starting-place. He tied up the boat, looked carefully round to see that he had left no traces behind him, and then turned to the water again. For a long time, as it seemed to the watchers, he stood there, very big, very silent, in the moonlight. At last he seemed satisfied. Whatever his secret was, he had hidden it; and so with a gentle sigh, as unmistakable to Antony as if he had heard it, Cayley turned away and vanished again as quietly as he had come.

Antony gave him three minutes, and stepped out from the trees. He waited there for Bill to join him.

"Six," whispered Bill.

Antony nodded.

"I'm going round to the front of the house. You

get back to your tree and watch, in case Cayley
comes again. Your bedroom is the left-hand end one,
and Cayley's the end but one? Is that right?"

Bill nodded.

"Right. Wait in hiding till I come back. I don't
know how long I shall be, but don't be impatient.
It will seem longer than it is." He patted Bill on
the shoulder, and with a smile and a nod of the
head he left him there.

What was in the bag? What could Cayley want
to hide other than a key or a revolver? Keys and
revolvers sink of themselves; no need to put them
in a bag first. What was in the bag? Something which
wouldn't sink of itself; something which needed to be
helped with stones before it would hide itself safely
in the mud.

Well, they would find that out. There was no
object in worrying about it now. Bill had a dirty
night's work in front of him. But where was the body
which Antony had expected so confidently or, if there
were no body, where was Mark?

More immediately, however, where was Cayley?
As quickly as he could Antony had got to the front
of the house and was now lying in the shrubbery
which bordered the lawn, waiting for the light to
go up in Cayley's window. If it went up in Bill's
window, then they were discovered. It would mean
that Cayley had glanced into Bill's room, had been
suspicious of the dummy figure in the bed, and had
turned up the light to make sure. After that, it was
war between them. But if it went up in Cayley's
room——

There was a light. Antony felt a sudden thrill of
excitement. It was in Bill's room. War!

The light stayed there, shining vividly, for a wind had come up, blowing the moon behind a cloud, and casting a shadow over the rest of the house. Bill had left his curtains undrawn. It was careless of him; the first stupid thing he had done, but——

The moon slipped out again . . . and Antony laughed to himself in the bushes. There was another window beyond Cayley's, and there was no light in it. The declaration of war was postponed.

Antony lay there, watching Cayley into bed. After all, it was only polite to return Cayley's own solicitude earlier in the night. Politeness demanded that one should not disport oneself on the pond until one's friends were comfortably tucked up.

Meanwhile Bill was getting tired of waiting. His chief fear was that he might spoil everything by forgetting the number "six." It was the sixth post. Six. He broke off a twig and divided it into six pieces. These he arranged on the ground in front of him. Six. He looked at the pond, counted up to the sixth post, and murmured "six" to himself again. Then he looked down at his twigs. One—two—three—four—five—six—seven. *Seven!* Was it seven? Or was that seventh bit of a twig an accidental bit which had been on the ground anyhow? Surely it was six! Had he said "six" to Antony? If so, Antony would remember, and it was all right. Six. He threw away the seventh twig and collected the other six together. Perhaps they would be safer in his pocket. Six. The height of a tall man—well, his own height. Six feet. Yes, that was the way to remember it. Feeling a little safer on the point, he began to wonder about the bag, and what Antony would say to it, and the possible depth of the water and of the mud at the bottom; and was still so wondering, and saying, "Good Lord, what a life!" to himself, when Antony reappeared.

Bill got up and came down the slope to meet him.

"Six," he said firmly. "Sixth post from the end."

"Good," smiled Antony. "Mine was the eighteenth —a little way past it."

"What did you go off for?"

"To see Cayley into bed."

"Is it all right?"

"Yes. Better hang your coat over the sixth post, and then we shall see it more easily. I'll put mine on the eighteenth. Are you going to undress here or in the boat?"

"Some here, and some in the boat. You're quite sure that you wouldn't like to do the diving yourself?"

"Quite, thanks."

They had walked round to the other side of the pond. Coming to the sixth post of the fence, Bill took off his coat and put it in position, and then finished his undressing, while Antony went off to mark the eighteenth post. When they were ready, they got into the boat, Antony taking the oars.

"Now, Bill, tell me as soon as I'm in a line with your two marks."

He rowed slowly towards the middle of the pond.

"You're about there now," said Bill at last.

Antony stopped rowing and looked about him.

"Yes, that's pretty well right." He turned the boat's nose round until it was pointing to the pine-tree under which Bill had lain. "You see my tree and the other coat?"

"Yes," said Bill.

"Right. Now then, I'm going to row gently along

this line until we're dead in between the two. Get
it as exact as you can—for your own sake."

"Steady!" said Bill warningly. "Back a little . . .
a little more . . . a little more forward again . . .
Right."

Antony left the oars on the water and looked
round. As far as he could tell, they were in an exact
line with each pair of landmarks.

"Now then, Bill, in you go."

Bill pulled off his shirt and trousers and stood up.

"You mustn't dive from the boat, old boy," caid
Antony hastily. "You'll shift its position. Slide in
gently."

Bill slid in from the stern and swam slowly round
to Antony.

"What's it like?" said Antony.

"Cold. Well, here's luck to it."

He gave a sudden kick, flashed for a moment in
the water, and was gone. Antony steadied the boat,
and took another look at his landmarks.

Bill came up behind him with a loud explosion.

"It's pretty muddy," he protested.

"Weeds?"

"No, thank the Lord."

"Well, try again."

Bill gave another kick and disappeared. Again
Antony coaxed the boat back into position, and again
Bill popped up, this time in front of him.

"I feel that if I threw you a sardine," said Antony, with a smile, "you'd catch it in your mouth
quite easily."

"It's awfully easy to be funny from where *you* are.
How much longer have I got to go on doing this?"

Antony looked at his watch.

"About three hours. We must get back before daylight. But be quicker if you can, because it's rather cold for me sitting here."

Bill flicked a handful of water at him and disappeared again. He was under for almost a minute this time, and there was a grin on his face when it was visible again.

"I've got it, but it's devilish hard to get up. I'm not sure that it isn't too heavy for me."

"That's all right," said Antony. He brought out a ball of thick string from his pocket. "Get this through the handle if you can, and then we can both pull."

"Good man." He paddled to the side, took one end of the string and paddled back again. "Now then."

Two minutes later the bag was safely in the boat. Bill clambered in after it, and Antony rowed back.

"Well done, Watson," he said quietly, as they landed.

He fetched their two coats, and then waited, the bag in his hand, while Bill dried and dressed himself. As soon as the latter was ready, he took his arm and led him into the copse. He put the bag down and felt in his pockets.

"I shall light a pipe before I open it," he said. "What about you?"

"Yes."

They sat down, and taking the bag between his knees, Antony pressed the catch and opened it.

"Clothes!" said Bill.

Antony pulled out the top garment and shook it out. It was a wet brown flannel coat.

"Do you recognize it?" he asked.

"Mark's brown flannel suit."

"The one he is advertised as having run away in?"

"Yes. It looks like it. Of course he had a dashed lot of clothes."

Antony put his hand in the breast-pocket and took out some letters. He considered them doubtfully for a moment.

"I suppose I'd better read them," he said. "I mean, just to see——" He looked inquiringly at Bill, who nodded. Antony turned on his torch and glanced at them. Bill waited anxiously.

"Yes. Mark. . . . Hallo!"

"What is it?"

"The letter that Cayley was telling the inspector about. From Robert. 'Mark, your loving brother is coming to see you——' Yes, I suppose I had better keep this. Well, that's his coat. Let's have out the rest of it." He took the remaining clothes from the bag and spread them out.

"They're all here," said Bill. "Shirt, tie, socks, underclothes, shoes—yes, all of them."

"All that he was wearing yesterday?"

"Yes."

"What do you make of it?"

Bill shook his head, and asked another question.

"Is it what you expected?"

Antony laughed suddenly.

"It's too absurd," he said. "I expected—well, you know what I expected. A body. A body in a suit of clothes. Well, perhaps it would be safer to hide them separately. The body here, and the clothes in the passage, where they would never betray themselves. And now he takes a great deal of trouble to hide the clothes here, and doesn't bother about the body at all." He shook his head. "I'm a bit lost for the moment, Bill, and that's the fact."

"Anything else there?"

Antony felt in the bag.

"Stones and—yes, there's something else." He took it out and held it up. "There we are, Bill."

It was the office key.

"By Jove, you were right."

Antony felt in the bag again, and then turned it gently upside down on the grass. A dozen large stones fell out—and something else. He flashed down his torch.

"Another key," he said.

He put the two keys in his pocket, and sat there for a long time in silence, thinking. Bill was silent, too, not liking to interrupt his thoughts, but at last he said:

"Shall I put these things back, Tony?"

Antony looked up with a start.

"What? Oh, yes. No, I'll put them back. You give me a light, will you?"

Very slowly and carefully he put the clothes back in the bag, pausing as he took up each garment, in the certainty, as it seemed to Bill, that it had something to tell him if only he could read it. When the last of them was inside, he still waited there on his knees, thinking.

"That's the lot," said Bill.

Antony nodded at him.

"Yes, that's the lot," he said; "and that's the funny thing about it. You're sure it is the lot?"

"What do you mean?"

"Give me the torch a moment." He took it and flashed it over the ground between them. "Yes, that's the lot. It's funny." He stood up, the bag in his hands. "Now let's find a hiding-place for these, and then——" He said no more, but stepped off through the trees, Bill following him meekly.

As soon as they had got the bag off their hands and were clear of the copse, Antony became more communicative. He took the two keys out of his pocket.

"One of them is the office key, I suppose, and the other is the key of the passage cupboard. So I thought that perhaps we might have a look at the cupboard."

"I say, do you really think it is?"

"Well, I don't see what else it can be."

"But why should he want to throw it away?"

"Because it has now done its work, whatever it was, and he wants to wash his hands of the passage. He'd throw the passage away if he could. I don't think it matters much one way or another, and I don't suppose there's anything to find in the cupboard, but I feel that we must look."

"Do you still think Mark's body might be there?"

"No. And yet where else can it be? Unless I'm hopelessly wrong and Cayley never killed him at all."

Bill hesitated, wondering if he dare advance his theory.

"I know you'll think me an ass——"

"My dear Bill, I'm such an obvious ass myself that I should be delighted to think you are too."

"Well, then suppose Mark did kill Robert, and Cayley helped him to escape, just as we thought at first. I know you proved afterwards that it was impossible, but suppose it happened in a way we don't know about and for reasons we don't know about. I mean, there are such a lot of funny things about the whole show that—well, almost anything might have happened."

"You're quite right. Well?"

"Well, then, this clothes business. Doesn't that seem rather to bear out the escaping theory? Mark's brown suit was known to the police. Couldn't Cayley have brought him another one in the passage, to escape in, and then have had the brown one on his hands? And thought it safest to hide it in the pond?"

"Yes," said Antony thoughtfully. And then: "Go on."

Bill went on eagerly:

"It all seems to fit in, you know. I mean even with your first theory—that Mark killed him accidentally and then came to Cayley for help. Of course, if Cayley had played fair, he'd have told Mark that he had nothing to be afraid of. But he isn't playing fair; he wants to get Mark out of the way because of the girl. Well, this is his chance. He makes Mark as frightened as possible, and tells him that his only hope is to run away. Well, naturally, he does all he can to get him well away, because if Mark is caught, the whole story of Cayley's treachery comes out."

"Yes. But isn't it overdoing it rather to make him change his underclothes and everything? It wastes a good deal of time, you know."

Bill was pulled up short, and said, "Oh!" in great disappointment.

"No, it's not as bad as that, Bill," said Antony with a smile. "I daresay the underclothes could be explained. But here's the difficulty. Why did Mark need to change from brown to blue, or whatever it was, when Cayley was the only person who saw him in brown?"

"The police description of him says that he is in a brown suit."

"Yes, because Cayley told the police. You see, even if Mark had had lunch in his brown suit, and the servants had noticed it, Cayley could always have pretended that he had changed into blue after lunch, because only Cayley saw him afterwards. So if Cayley had told the inspector that he was wearing blue, Mark could have escaped quite comfortably in his brown, without needing to change at all."

"But that's just what he did do," cried Bill triumphantly. "What fools we are!"

Antony looked at him in surprise, and then shook his head.

"Yes, yes!" insisted Bill. "Of course! Don't you see? Mark did change after lunch, and, to give him more of a chance of getting away, Cayley lied and said that he was wearing the brown suit in which the servants had seen him. Well, then he was afraid that the police might examine Mark's clothes and find the brown suit still there, so he hid it, and then dropped it in the pond afterwards."

He turned eagerly to his friend, but Antony said nothing. Bill began to speak again, and was promptly waved into silence.

"Don't say anything more, old boy; you've given me quite enough to think about. Don't let's bother about it to-night. We'll just have a look at this cupboard and then get to bed."

But the cupboard had not much to tell them that night. It was empty save for a few old bottles.

"Well, that's that," said Bill.

But Antony, on his knees with the torch in his hand, continued to search for something.

"What are you looking for?" asked Bill at last.

"Something that isn't there," said Antony, getting up and dusting his trousers. And he locked the door again.

CHAPTER XVIII

GUESS-WORK

The inquest was at three o'clock; thereafter Antony could have no claim on the hospitality of the Red House. By ten o'clock his bag was packed, and waiting to be taken to the "George." To Bill, coming upstairs after a more prolonged breakfast, this early morning bustle was a little surprising.

"What's the hurry?" he asked.

"None. But we don't want to come back here after the inquest. Get your packing over now and then we can have the morning to ourselves."

"Righto." He turned to go to his room, and then come back again. "I say, are we going to tell Cayley that we're staying at the 'George'?"

"You're not staying at the 'George,' Bill. Not officially. You're going to London."

"Oh!"

"Yes. Ask Cayley to have your luggage sent in to Stanton, ready for you to catch a train there after the inquest. You can tell him that you've got to see the Bishop of London at once. The fact that you are hurrying back to London to be confirmed will make it seem more natural that I should resume my interrupted solitude at the 'George' as soon as you have gone."

"Then where do I sleep tonight?"

"Officially, I suppose, in Fulham Palace; unofficially, I suspect, in my bed, unless they've got another spare room at the 'George.' I've put in your confirmation robe—I mean your pyjamas and brushes and things—in my bag, ready for you. Is there anything else you want to know? No? Then go and pack. And meet me at ten-thirty beneath the blasted oak or in the hall or somewhere. I want to talk and talk and talk, and I must have my Watson."

"Good," said Bill, and went off to his room.

An hour later, having communicated their official plans to Cayley, they wandered out together into the park.

"Well?" said Bill, as they sat down underneath a convenient tree. "Talk away."

"I had many bright thoughts in my bath this morning," began Antony. "The brightest one of all was that we were being damn fools, and working at this thing from the wrong end altogether."

"Well, that's a helpful thought."

"Of course it's very hampering being a detective, when you don't know anything about detecting, and when nobody knows that you're doing detection, and you can't have people up to cross-examine them, and you have neither the energy nor the means to make proper inquiries; and, in short, when you're doing the whole thing in a thoroughly amateur, haphazard way."

"For amateurs I don't think we're doing at all badly," protested Bill.

"No; not for amateurs. But if we had been professionals, I believe we should have gone at it from the other end. The Robert end. We've been wondering about Mark and Cayley all the time. Now let's wonder about Robert for a bit."

"We know so little about him."

"Well, let's see what we do know. First of all, then, we know vaguely that he was a bad lot—the sort of brother who is hushed up in front of other people."

"Yes."

"We know that he announced his approaching arrival to Mark in a rather unpleasant letter, which I have in my pocket."

"Yes."

"And then we know rather a curious thing. We know that Mark told you all that this black sheep was coming. Now, why did he tell you?"

Bill was thoughtful for a moment.

"I suppose," he said slowly, "that he knew we were bound to see him, and thought that the best way was to be quite frank about him."

"But were you bound to see him? You were all away playing golf."

"Very well, then. That's one thing we've discovered. Mark knew that Robert was staying in the house that night. Or shall we put it this way—he knew that there was no chance of getting Robert out of the house at once."

Bill looked at his friend eagerly.

"Go on," he said. "This is getting interesting."

"He also knew something else," went on Antony. "He knew that Robert was bound to betray his real character to you as soon as you met him. He couldn't pass him off on you as just a travelled brother from the Dominions, with perhaps a bit of an accent; he had to tell you at once, because you were bound to find out, that Robert was a wastrel."

"Yes. That's sound enough."

"Well, now, doesn't it strike you that Mark made up his mind about all that rather quickly?"

"How do you mean?"

"He got this letter at breakfast. He read it; and directly he had read it he began to confide in you all. That is to say, in about one second he thought out the whole business and came to a decision—to two decisions. He considered the possibility of getting Robert out of the way before you came back, and decided that it was impossible. He considered the possibility of Robert's behaving like an ordinary decent person in public, and decided that it was very unlikely. He came to those two decisions instantaneously, as he was reading the letter. Isn't that rather quick work?"

"Well, what's the explanation?"

Antony waited until he had refilled and lighted his pipe before answering.

"What's the explanation? Well, let's leave it for a moment and take another look at the two brothers. In conjunction, this time, with Mrs. Norbury."

"Mrs. Norbury?" said Bill, surprised.

"Yes. Mark hoped to marry Miss Norbury. Now, if Robert really was a blot upon the family honour, Mark would want to do one of two things. Either keep it from the Norburys altogether, or else, if it had to come out, tell them himself before the news came to them indirectly. Well, he told them. But the funny thing is that he told them the day before Robert's letter came. Robert came, and was killed, the day before yesterday—Tuesday. Mark told Mrs. Norbury about him on Monday. What do you make of that?"

"Coincidence," said Bill, after careful thought. "He'd always meant to tell her; his suit was prospering, and just before it was finally settled, he told her. That happened to be Monday. On Tuesday he got Robert's letter, and felt jolly glad that he'd told her in time."

"Well, it might be that, but it's rather a curious coincidence. And here is something which makes it very curious indeed. It only occurred to me in the bath this morning. Inspiring place, a bathroom. Well, it's this—he told her on Monday morning, on his way to Middleston in the car."

"Well?"

"Well."

"Sorry, Tony; I'm dense this morning."

"In the car, Bill. And how near can the car get to Jallands?"

"About six hundred yards."

"Yes. And on his way to Middleston, on some business or other, Mark stops the car, walks six hundred yards down the hill to Jallands, says, 'Oh, by the way, Mrs. Norbury, I don't think I ever told you that I have a shady brother called Robert,' walks six hundred yards up the hill again, gets into the car, and goes off to Middleston. Is that likely?"

Bill frowned heavily.

"Yes, but I don't see what you're getting at. Likely or not likely, we know he did do it."

"Of course he did. All I mean is that he must have had some strong reason for telling Mrs. Norbury at once. And the reason I suggest is that he knew on that morning—Monday morning, not Tuesday—that Robert was coming to see him, and had to be in first with the news."

"But—but——"

"And that would explain the other point—his instantaneous decision at breakfast to tell you all about his brother. It wasn't instantaneous. He knew on

Monday that Robert was coming, and decided then that you would all have to know."

"Then how do you explain the letter?"

"Well, let's have a look at it."

Antony took the letter from his pocket and spread it out on the grass between them.

"*Mark, your loving brother is coming to see you to-morrow, all the way from Australia. I give you warning so that you will be able to conceal your surprise but not I hope your pleasure. Expect him at three or thereabouts.*"

"No date mentioned, you see," said Antony. "Just 'to-morrow.'"

"But he got this on Tuesday."

"Did he?"

"Well, he read it out to us on Tuesday."

"Oh, yes! he read it out to you."

Bill read the letter again, and then turned it over and looked at the back of it. The back of it had nothing to say to him.

"What about the postmark?" he asked.

"We haven't got the envelope, unfortunately."

"And you think that he got this letter on Monday."

"I'm inclined to think so, Bill. Anyhow, I think —I feel almost certain—that he knew on Monday that his brother was coming."

"Is that going to help us much?"

"No. It makes it more difficult. There's something rather uncanny about it all. I don't understand it." He was silent for a little, and then added, "I wonder if the inquest is going to help us."

"What about last night? I'm longing to hear what you make of that. Have you been thinking it out at all?"

"Last night," said Antony thoughtfully to himself. "Yes, last night wants some explaining."

Bill waited hopefully for him to explain. What, for instance, had Antony been looking for in the cupboard?

"I think," began Antony slowly, "that after last night we must give up the idea that Mark has been killed; killed, I mean, by Cayley. I don't believe anybody would go to so much trouble to hide a suit of clothes when he had a body on his hands. The body would seem so much more important. I think we may take it now that the clothes are all that Cayley had to hide."

"But why not have kept them in the passage?"

"He was frightened of the passage. Miss Norris knew about it."

"Well, then, in his own bedroom, or even in Mark's. For all you or I or anybody knew, Mark might have had two brown suits. He probably had, I should think."

"Probably. But I doubt if that would reassure Cayley. The brown suit hid a secret, and therefore the brown suit had to be hidden. We all know that in theory the safest hiding-place is the most obvious, but in practice very few people have the nerve to risk it."

Bill looked rather disappointed.

"Then we just come back to where we were," he complained. "Mark killed his brother, and Cayley helped him to escape through the passage; either in order to compromise him, or because there was no other way out of it. And he helped him by telling a lie about his brown suit."

Antony smiled at him in genuine amusement.

"Bad luck, Bill," he said sympathetically. "There's

only one murder, after all. I'm awfully sorry about it. It was my fault for——"

"Shut up, you ass. You know I didn't mean that."

"Well, you seemed awfully disappointed."

Bill said nothing for a little, and then with a sudden laugh confessed.

"It was so exciting yesterday," he said apologetically, "and we seemed to be just getting there, and discovering the most wonderful things, and now——"

"And now?"

"Well, it's so much more ordinary."

Antony gave a shout of laughter.

"Ordinary!" he cried. "Ordinary! Well, I'm dashed! Ordinary! If only *one* thing would happen in an ordinary way, we might do something, but *everything* is ridiculous."

Bill brightened up again.

"Ridiculous? How?"

"Every way. Take those ridiculous clothes we found last night. You can explain the brown suit, but why the underclothes. You can explain the underclothes in some absurd way, if you like—you can say that Mark always changed his underclothes whenever he interviewed anybody from Australia—but why, in that case, my dear Watson, *why* didn't he change his collar?"

"His collar?" said Bill in amazement.

"His collar, Watson."

"I don't understand."

"And it's all so ordinary," scoffed Antony.

"Sorry, Tony, I didn't mean that. Tell me about the collar."

"Well, that's all. There was no collar in the bag last night. Shirt, socks, tie—everything except a collar. Why?"

"Was that what you were looking for in the cupboard?" said Bill eagerly.

"Of course. 'Why no collar?' I said. For some reason Cayley considered it necessary to hide all Mark's clothes; not just the suit, but everything which he was wearing, or supposed to be wearing, at the time of the murder. But he hadn't hidden the collar. Why? Had he left it out by mistake? So I looked in the cupboard. It wasn't there. Had he left it out on purpose? If so, why—and where was it? Naturally I began to say to myself, 'Where have I seen a collar lately? A collar all by itself?' And I remembered—what, Bill?"

Bill frowned heavily to himself, and shook his head.

"Don't ask me, Tony. I can't—By Jove!" He threw up his head. "In the basket in the office bedroom!"

"Exactly."

"But is that the one?"

"The one that goes with the rest of the clothes? I don't know. Where else can it be? But if so, why send the collar quite casually to the wash in the ordinary way, and take immense trouble to hide every thing else? Why, why, why?"

Bill bit hard at his pipe, but could think of nothing to say.

"Anyhow," said Antony, getting up restlessly, "I'm certain of one thing. Mark knew on the Monday that Robert was coming here."

CHAPTER XIX

THE INQUEST

The Coroner, having made a few commonplace remarks as to the terrible nature of the tragedy which they had come to investigate that afternoon, proceeded to outline the case to the jury. Witnesses would be called to identify the deceased as Robert Ablett, the brother of the owner of the Red House, Mark Ablett. It would be shown that he was something of a ne'er-do-well, who had spent most of his life in Australia, and that he had announced, in what might almost be called a threatening letter, his intention of visiting his brother that afternoon. There would be evidence of his arrival, of his being shown into the scene of the tragedy—a room in the Red House, commonly called "the office"—and of his brother's entrance into the room. The jury would have to form their own opinion as to what happened there. But whatever happened, happened almost instantaneously. Within two minutes of Mark Ablett's entrance, as would be shown in the evidence, a shot was heard, and when—perhaps five minutes later—the room was forced open, the dead body of Robert Ablett was found stretched upon the floor. As regards Mark Ablett, nobody had seen him from the moment of his going into the room, but evidence would be called to show that he had enough money on him at the time to take him to any other part of the country, and that a man answering to his description had been observed on the platform of Stanton station, apparently waiting to catch the 8:55 up train to London. As the jury would realize, such evidence of identity was not always reliable. Missing men had a way of being seen in a dozen different places at once. In any case, there was no doubt that for the moment Mark Ablett had disappeared.

"Seems a sound man," whispered Antony to Bill, and Bill nodded. "Doesn't talk too much."

Antony did not expect to learn much from the evidence—he knew the facts of the case so well by now—but he wondered if Inspector Birch had developed any new theories. If so, they would appear in the Coroner's examination, for the Coroner would certainly have been coached by the police as to the important facts to be extracted from each witness. Bill was the first to be put through it.

"Now about this letter, Mr. Beverley?" he was asked when his chief evidence was over. "Did you see it at all?"

"I didn't see the actual writing. I saw the back of it. Mark was holding it up when he told us about his brother."

"You don't know what was in it, then?"

Bill had a sudden shock. He had read the letter only that morning. He knew quite well what was in it. But it wouldn't do to admit this. And then, just as he was about to perjure himself, he remembered: Antony had heard Cayley telling the inspector.

"I knew afterwards. I was told. But Mark didn't read it out at breakfast."

"You gathered, however, that it was an unwelcome letter?"

"Oh, yes!"

"Would you say that Mark was frightened by it?"

"Not frightened. Sort of bitter—and resigned. Sort of 'Oh, Lord, here we are again!' "

There was a titter here and there. The Coroner smiled, and tried to pretend that he hadn't.

"Thank you, Mr. Beverley."

The next witness was summoned by the name of Andrew Amos, and Antony looked up with interest, wondering who it was.

"He lives at the inner lodge," whispered Bill to him.

All that Amos had to say was that a stranger had passed by his lodge at a little before three that afternoon, and had spoken to him. He had seen the body and recognized it as the man.

"What did he say?"

" 'Is this right for the Red House?' or something like that, sir."

"What did you say?"

"I said, 'This is the Red House. Who do you want to see?' He was a bit rough-looking, you know, sir, and I didn't know what he was doing there."

"Well?"

"Well, sir, he said, 'Is Mister Mark Ablett at home?' It doesn't sound much put like that, sir, but I didn't care about the way he said it. So I got in front of him like, and said, 'What do you want, eh?' and he gave a sort of chuckle and said, 'I want to see my dear brother Mark.' Well, then I took a closer look at him, and I see that p'raps he might be his brother, so I said, 'If you'll follow the drive, sir, you'll come to the house. Of course I can't say if Mr. Ablett's at home.' And he gave a sort of nasty laugh again, and said, 'Fine place Mister Mark Ablett's got here. Plenty of money to spend, eh?' Well, then I had another look at him, sir, because gentlemen don't talk like that, and if he was Mr. Ablett's brother—but before I could make up my mind, he laughed and went on. That's all I can tell you, sir."

Andrew Amos stepped down and moved away to the back of the room, nor did Antony take his eyes off him until he was assured that Amos intended to remain there until the inquest was over.

"Who's Amos talking to now?" he whispered to Bill.

"Parsons. One of the gardeners. He's at the outside lodge on the Stanton road. They're all here to-day. Sort of holiday for 'em."

"I wonder if he's giving evidence too," thought Antony.

He was. He followed Amos. He had been at work on the lawn in front of the house, and had seen Robert Ablett arrive. He didn't hear the shot—not to notice. He was a little hard of hearing. He had seen a gentleman arrive about five minutes after Mr. Robert.

"Can you see him in court now?" asked the Coroner.

Parsons looked round slowly. Antony caught his eye and smiled.

"That's him," said Parsons, pointing.

Everybody looked at Antony.

"That was about five minutes afterwards?"

"About that, sir."

"Did anybody come out of the house before this gentleman's arrival?"

"No, sir. That is to say, I didn't see 'em."

Stevens followed. She gave her evidence much as she had given it to the inspector. Nothing new was brought out by her examination. Then came Elsie. As the reporters scribbled down what she had overheard, they added in brackets *"Sensation"* for the first time that afternoon.

"How soon after you had heard this did the shot come?" asked the Coroner.

"Almost at once, sir."

"A minute?"

"I couldn't really say, sir. It was so quick."

"Were you still in the hall?"

"Oh, no, sir. I was just outside Mrs. Stevens' room. The housekeeper, sir."

"You didn't think of going back to the hall to see what had happened?"

"Oh, no, sir. I just went in to Mrs. Stevens, and she said, 'Oh, what was that?' frightened-like. And I said, 'That was in the house, Mrs. Stevens, that was.' Just like something going off, it was."

"Thank you," said the Coroner.

There was another emotional disturbance in the room as Cayley went into the witness-box; not *"Sensation"* this time, but an eager and, as it seemed to Antony, sympathetic interest. Now they were getting to grips with the drama.

He gave his evidence carefully, unemotionally—the lies with the same slow deliberation as the truth. Antony watched him intently, wondering what it was about him which had this odd sort of attractiveness. For Antony, who knew that he was lying, and lying (as he believed) not for Mark's sake but his own, yet could not help sharing some of that general sympathy with him.

"Was Mark ever in possession of a revolver?" asked the Coroner.

"Not to my knowledge. I think I should have known if he had been."

"You were alone with him all that morning. Did he talk about this visit of Robert's at all?"

"I didn't see very much of him in the morning. I was at work in my room, and outside, and so on. We lunched together and he talked of it then a little."

"In what terms?"

"Well——" he hesitated, and then went on, "I can't think of a better word than 'peevishly.' Occasionally he said, 'What do you think he wants?' or 'Why couldn't he have stayed where he was?' or 'I don't like the tone of his letter. Do you think he means trouble?' He talked rather in that kind of way."

"Did he express his surprise that his brother should be in England?"

"I think he was always afraid that he would turn up one day."

"Yes. . . . You didn't hear any conversation between the brothers when they were in the office together?"

"No. I happened to go into the library just after Mark had gone in, and I was there all the time."

"Was the library door open?"

"Oh, yes."

"Did you see or hear the last witness at all?"

"No."

"If anybody had come out of the office while you were in the library, would you have heard it?"

"I think so. Unless they had come out very quietly on purpose."

"Yes. . . . Would you call Mark a hasty-tempered man?"

Cayley considered this carefully before answering.

"Hasty-tempered, yes," he said. "But not violent-tempered."

"Was he fairly athletic? Active and quick?"

"Active and quick, yes. Not particularly strong."

"Yes. . . . One question more. Was Mark in the habit of carrying any considerable sum of money about with him?"

"Yes. He always had one £100 note on him, and perhaps ten or twenty pounds as well."

"Thank you, Mr. Cayley."

Cayley went back heavily to his seat. "Damn it," said Antony to himself, "why do I like the fellow?"

"Antony Gillingham!"

Again the eager interest of the room could be felt. Who was this stranger who had got mixed up in the business so mysteriously?

Antony smiled at Bill and stepped up to give his evidence.

He explained how he came to be staying at the "George" at Woodham, how he had heard that the Red House was in the neighborhood, how he had walked over to see his friend Beverley, and had arrived just after the tragedy. Thinking it over afterwards he was fairly certain that he had heard the shot, but it had not made any impression on him at the time. He had come to the house from the Woodham end and consequently had seen nothing of Robert Ablett, who had been a few minutes in front of him. From this point his evidence coincided with Cayley's.

"You and the last witness reached the French windows together and found them shut?"

"Yes."

"You pushed them in and came to the body. Of course you had no idea whose body it was?"

"No."

"Did Mr. Cayley say anything?"

"He turned the body over, just so as to see the face, and when he saw it, he said, 'Thank God.'"

Again the reporters wrote *"Sensation."*

"Did you understand what he meant by that?"

"I asked him who it was, and he said that it was Robert Ablett. Then he explained that he was afraid at first it was the cousin with whom he lived—Mark."

"Yes. Did he seem upset?"

"Very much so at first. Less when he found that it wasn't Mark."

There was a sudden snigger from a nervous gentleman in the crowd at the back of the room, and the Coroner put on his glasses and stared sternly in the direction from which it came. The nervous gentleman hastily decided that the time had come to do up his bootlace. The Coroner put down his glasses and continued.

"Did anybody come out of the house while you were coming up the drive?"

"No."

"Thank you, Mr. Gillingham."

He was followed by Inspector Birch. The Inspector, realizing that this was his afternoon, and that the eyes of the world were upon him, produced a plan of the house and explained the situation of the different rooms. The plan was then handed to the jury.

Inspector Birch, so he told the world, had arrived at the Red House at 4:42 p.m. on the afternoon in question. He had been received by Mr. Matthew Cayley, who had made a short statement to him, and he had then proceeded to examine the scene of the crime. The French windows had been forced from outside. The door leading into the hall was locked;

he had searched the room thoroughly and had found no trace of a key. In the bedroom leading out of the office he had found an open window. There were no marks on the window, but it was a low one, and, as he found from experiment, quite easy to step out of without touching it with the boots. A few yards outside the window a shrubbery began. There were no recent footmarks outside the window, but the ground was in a very hard condition owing to the absence of rain. In the shrubbery, however, he found several twigs on the ground, recently broken off, together with other evidence that somebody had been forcing its way through. He had questioned everybody connected with the estate, and none of them had been into the shrubbery recently. By forcing a way through the shrubbery it was possible for a person to make a detour of the house and get to the Stanton end of the park without ever being in sight of the house itself.

He had made inquiries about the deceased. Deceased had left for Australia some fifteen years ago, owing to some financial trouble at home. Deceased was not well spoken of in the village from which he and his brother had come. Deceased and his brother had never been on good terms, and the fact that Mark Ablett had come into money had been a cause of great bitterness between them. It was shortly after this that Robert had left for Australia.

He had made inquiries at Stanton station. It had been market-day at Stanton and the station had been more full of arrivals than usual. Nobody had particularly noticed the arrival of Robert Ablett; there had been a good many passengers by the 2:10 train that afternoon, the train by which Robert had undoubtedly come from London. A witness, however, would state that he noticed a man resembling Mark Ablett at the station at 3:53 p.m. that afternoon and that this man caught the 3:55 up train to town.

There was a pond in the grounds of the Red House. He had dragged this, but without result. . . .

Antony listened to him carelessly, thinking his own thoughts all the time. Medical evidence followed, but there was nothing to be got from that. He felt so close to the truth; at any moment something might give his brain the one little hint which it wanted. Inspector Birch was just pursuing the ordinary. Whatever else this case was, it was not ordinary. There was something uncanny about it.

John Borden was giving evidence. He was on the up platform seeing a friend off by the 3:55 on Tuesday afternoon. He had noticed a man on the platform with coat-collar turned up and a scarf round his chin. He had wondered why the man should do this on such a hot day. The man seemed to be trying to escape observation. Directly the train came in, he hurried into a carriage. And so on.

"There's always a John Borden at every murder case," said Antony to himself.

"Have you ever seen Mark Ablett?"

"Once or twice, sir."

"Was it he?"

"I never really got a good look at him, sir, what with his collar turned up and the scarf and all. But directly I heard of the sad affair, and that Mr. Ablett was missing, I said to Mrs. Borden, 'Now I wonder if that was Mr. Ablett I saw at the station?' So then we talked it over and decided that I ought to come and tell Inspector Birch. It was just Mr. Ablett's height, sir."

Antony went on with his thoughts. . . .

The Coroner was summing up. The jury, he said, had now heard all the evidence and would have to decide what had happened in that room between the two brothers. How had the deceased met his death? The medical evidence would probably satisfy them that Robert Ablett had died from the effects of a bullet-wound in the head. Who had fired that bullet? If Robert Ablett had fired it himself, no doubt they would bring in a verdict of suicide, but if this had been so, where was the revolver which had fired it, and what had become of Mark Ablett? If they disbelieved in this possibility of suicide, what remained? Accidental death, justifiable homicide, and murder. Could the deceased have been killed accidentally? It was possible, but then would Mark Ablett have run away? The evidence that he had run away from the scene of the crime was strong. His cousin had seen him go into the room, the servant Elsie Wood had heard him quarrelling with his brother in the room, the door had been locked from the inside, and there were signs that outside the open window someone had pushed his way very recently through the shrubbery. Who, if not Mark? They would have then to consider whether he would have run away if he had been guiltless of his brother's death. No doubt innocent people lost their heads sometimes. It was possible that if it were proved afterwards that Mark Ablett had shot his brother, it might also be proved that he was justified in so doing, and that when he ran away from his brother's corpse he had really nothing to fear at the hands of the Law. In this connexion he need hardly remind the jury that they were not the final tribunal, and that if they found Mark

Ablett guilty of murder, it would not prejudice his trial in any way, if and when he was apprehended. . . . The jury could consider their verdict.

They considered it. They announced that the deceased had died as the result of a bullet-wound, and that the bullet had been fired by his brother Mark Ablett.

Bill turned round to Antony at his side. But Antony was gone. Across the room he saw Andrew Amos and Parsons going out of the door together, and Antony was between them.

CHAPTER XX

MR. BEVERLEY IS TACTFUL

The inquest had been held at the "Lamb" at Stanton; at Stanton Robert Ablett was to be buried next day. Bill waited about outside for his friend, wondering where he had gone. Then realizing that Cayley would be coming out to his car directly, and that a farewell talk with Cayley would be a little embarrassing, he wandered round to the yard at the back of the inn, lit a cigarette, and stood surveying a torn and weather-beaten poster on the stable wall. "GRAND THEATRICAL ENTER" it announced, to take place on "Wednesday, Decem." Bill smiled to himself as he looked at it, for the part of Joe, a loquacious postman, had been played by "William B. Beverl," as the remnants of the poster still maintained, and he had been much less loquacious than the author had intended, having forgotten his words completely, but it had all been great fun. And then he stopped smiling, for there would be no more fun now at the Red House.

"Sorry to keep you waiting," said the voice of Antony behind him. "My old friends Amos and Parsons insisted on giving me a drink."

He slipped his hand into the crook of Bill's arm, and smiled happily at him.

"Why were you so keen about them?" asked Bill

a little resentfully. "I couldn't think where on earth you had got to."

Antony didn't say anything. He was staring at the poster.

"When did this happen?" he asked.

"What?"

Antony waved to the poster.

"Oh, that? Last Christmas. It was rather fun."

Antony began to laugh to himself.

"Were you good?"

"Rotten. I don't profess to be an actor."

"Mark good?"

"Oh, rather. He loves it."

"Rev. Henry Stutters—Mr. Matthew Cay," read Antony. "Was that our friend Cayley?"

"Yes."

"Any good?"

"Well, much better than I expected. He wasn't keen, but Mark made him."

"Miss Norris wasn't playing, I see.

"My dear Tony, she's a professional. Of course she wasn't."

Antony laughed again.

"A green success, was it?"

"Oh, rather!"

"I'm a fool, and a damned fool," Antony announced solemnly. "And a damned fool," he said again under his breath, as he led Bill away from the poster, and out of the yard into the road. "And a damned fool. Even now——" He broke off and then asked suddenly, "Did Mark ever have much trouble with his teeth?"

"He went to his dentist a good deal. But what on earth——"

Antony laughed a third time.

"What luck!" he chuckled. "But how do you know?"

"We go to the same man; Mark recommended him to me. Cartwright, in Wimpole Street."

"Cartwright in Wimpole Street," repeated Antony thoughtfully. "Yes, I can remember that. Cartwright in Wimpole Street. Did Cayley go to him too, by any chance?"

"I expect so. Oh, yes, I know he did. But what on earth——"

"What was Mark's general health like? Did he see a doctor much?"

"Hardly at all, I should think. He did a lot of early morning exercises which were supposed to make him bright and cheerful at breakfast. They didn't do that, but they seemed to keep him pretty fit. Tony, I wish you'd——"

Antony held up a hand and hushed him into silence.

"One last question," he said. "Was Mark fond of swimming?"

"No, he hated it. I don't believe he *could* swim. Tony, are you mad, or am I? Or is this a new game?"

Antony squeezed his arm.

"Dear old Bill," he said. "It's a game. What a game! And the answer is Cartwright in Wimpole Street."

They walked in silence for half a mile or so along the road to Woodham. Bill tried two or three times to get his friend to talk, but Antony had only grunted in reply. He was just going to make another attempt, when Antony came to a sudden stop and turned to him anxiously.

"I wonder if you'd do something for me, Bill," he said, looking at him with some doubt.

"What sort of thing?"

"Well, it's really dashed important. It's just the one thing I want now."

Bill was suddenly enthusiastic again.

"I say, have you really found it all out?"

Antony nodded.

"At least, I'm very nearly there. There's just this one thing I want now. It means your going back to Stanton. Well, we haven't come far; it won't take you long. Do you mind?"

"My dear Holmes, I am at your service."

Antony gave him a smile and was silent for a little thinking.

"Is there another inn at Stanton—fairly close to the station?"

"The 'Plough and Horses'—just at the corner where the road goes up to the station—is that the one you mean?"

"That would be the one. I suppose you could do with a drink, couldn't you?"

"Rather!" said Bill with a grin.

"Good. Then have one at the 'Plough and Horses.' Have two, if you like, and talk to the landlord, or landlady, or whoever serves you. I want you to find out if anybody stayed there on Monday night."

"Robert?" said Bill eagerly.

"I didn't say Robert," said Antony, smiling. "I just want you to find out if they had a visitor who slept there on Monday night. A stranger. If so, then any particulars you can get of him, without letting the landlord know that you are interested—"

"Leave it to me," broke in Bill. "I know just what you want."

"Don't assume that it was Robert—or anybody else. Let *them* describe the man to you. Don't influence them unconsciously by suggesting that he was

short or tall, or anything of that sort. Just get them
talking. If it's the landlord, you'd better stand him
a drink or two."

"Right you are," said Bill confidently. "Where do
I meet you again?"

"Probably at the 'George.' If you get there before
me, you can order dinner for eight o'clock. Anyhow
we'll meet at eight, if not before."

"Good." He nodded to Antony and strode off back
to Stanton again.

Antony stood watching him with a little smile at
his enthusiasm. Then he looked round slowly,
as if in search of something. Suddenly he saw what
he wanted. Twenty yards farther on a lane wandered
off to the left, and there was a gate a little way up
on the right-hand side of it. Antony walked to the
gate filling his pipe as he went. Then he lit his pipe,
sat on the gate, and took his head in his hands.

"Now then," he said to himself, "let's begin at the
beginning."

It was nearly eight o'clock when William Beverley,
the famous sleuth-hound, arrived, tired and dusty, at
the "George," to find Antony, cool and clean, standing bare-headed at the door, waiting for him.

"Is dinner ready?" were Bill's first words.

"Yes."

"Then I'll just have a wash. Lord, I'm tired."

"I never ought to have asked you," said Antony
penitently.

"That's all right. I shan't be a moment." Half-
way up the stairs he turned round and asked, "Am I
in your room?"

"Yes. Do you know the way?"

"Yes. Start carving, will you? And order lots of

beer." He disappeared round the top of the staircase. Antony went slowly in.

When the first edge of his appetite had worn off, and he was able to spare a little time between the mouthfuls, Bill gave an account of his adventures. The landlord of the "Plough and Horses" had been sticky, decidedly sticky—Bill had been unable at first to get anything out of him. But Bill had been tactful; lorblessyou, how tactful he had been.

"He kept on about the inquest, and what a queer affair it had been, and so on, and how there'd been an inquest in his wife's family once, which he seemed rather proud about, and I kept saying, 'Pretty busy, I suppose, just now, what?' and then he'd say 'Middlin',' and go on again about Susan—that was the one that had the inquest—he talked about it as if it were a disease—and then I'd try again, and say, 'Slack times, I expect, just now, eh?' and he'd say 'Middlin'' again, and then it was time to offer him another drink, and I didn't seem to be getting much nearer. But I got him at last. I asked him if he knew John Borden—he was the man who said he'd seen Mark at the station. Well, he knew all about Borden, and after he'd told me all about Borden's wife's family, and how one of them had been burnt to death—after you with the beer; thanks—well, then I said carelessly that it must be very hard to remember anybody whom you had just seen once, so as to identify him afterwards, and he agreed that it would be 'middlin' hard,' and then——"

"Give me three guesses," interrupted Antony. "You asked him if he remembered everybody who came to his inn?"

"That's it. Bright, wasn't it?"

"Brilliant. And what was the result?"

"The result was a woman."

"A woman?" said Antony eagerly.

"A woman," said Bill impressively. "Of course I thought it was going to be Robert—so did you, didn't you?—but it wasn't. It was a woman. Came quite late on Monday night in a car—driving herself—went off early next morning."

"Did he describe her?"

"Yes. She was middlin'. Middlin' tall, middlin' age, middlin' colour, and so on. Doesn't help much, does it? But still—a woman. Does that upset your theory?"

Antony shook his head.

"No, Bill, not at all," he said.

"You knew all the time? At least, you guessed?"

"Wait till to-morrow. I'll tell you everything to-morrow."

"To-morrow!" said Bill in great disappointment.

"Well, I'll tell you one thing to-night, if you'll promise not to ask any more questions. But you probably know it already."

"What is it?"

"Only that Mark Ablett did not kill his brother."

"And Cayley did?"

"That's another question, Bill. However, the answer is that Cayley didn't, either."

"Then who on earth——"

"Have some more beer," said Antony with a smile. And Bill had to be content with that.

They were early to bed that evening, for both of them were tired. Bill slept loudly and defiantly, but Antony lay awake, wondering. What was happening at the Red House now? Perhaps he would hear in the morning; perhaps he would get a letter. He went over the whole story again from the beginning—was there any possibility of a mistake? What would the police do? Would they ever find out? Ought he to have told them? Well, let them find out; it was their job. Surely he couldn't have made a mistake this time. No good wondering now; he would know definitely in the morning.

In the morning there was a letter for him.

CHAPTER XXI

CAYLEY'S APOLOGY

"My dear Mr. Gillingham,

"I gather from your letter that you have made certain discoveries which you may feel it your duty to communicate to the police, and that in this case my arrest on a charge of murder would inevitably follow. Why, in these circumstances, you should give me such ample warning of your intentions I do not understand, unless it is that you are not wholly out of sympathy with me. But whether or not you sympathize, at any rate you will want to know—and I want you to know—exactly what happened in the office on that afternoon, and the reasons which made this killing necessary. If the police have to be told anything, I would rather that they too knew the whole story. They, and even you, may call it murder, but by that time I shall be out of the way. Let them call it what they like.

"I must begin by taking you back to a summer day fifteen years ago, when I was a boy of thirteen and Mark a young man of twenty-five. His whole life was make-believe, and just now he was pretending to be a philanthropist. He sat in our little drawing-room, flicking his gloves against the back of his left hand, and my mother, good soul, thought what a noble young gentleman he was, and Philip and I, hastily washed and crammed into collars, stood in front of him, nudging each other and kicking the backs of our heels and cursing him in our hearts for having interrupted our game. He had decided to adopt one of us, kind Cousin Mark. Heaven knows why he chose *me*. Philip was eleven; two years longer to wait. Perhaps that was why.

"Well, Mark educated me. I went to a public school and to Cambridge, and I became his secretary. Well, much more than his secretary, as your friend Beverley perhaps has told you: his land agent, his financial adviser, his courier, his—but this most of all— his audience. Mark could never live alone. There must always be somebody to listen to him. I think in his heart he hoped I should be his Boswell. He told me one day that he had made me his literary executor— poor devil. And he used to write me the absurdest long letters when I was away from him, letters which I read once and then tore up. The futility of the man!

"It was three years ago that Philip got into trouble. He had been hurried through a cheap grammar school and into a London office, and discovered there that there was not much fun to be got in this world on two pounds a week. I had a frantic letter from him one day, saying that he must have a hundred at once, or he would be ruined, and I went to Mark for the money. Only to borrow it, you understand; he gave me a good salary and I could have paid it back in three months. But no. He saw nothing for himself in it, I suppose; no applause, no admiration. Philip's gratitude would be to me, not to him. I begged, I threatened, we argued; and while we were arguing, Philip was arrested. It killed my mother—he was always her favourite—but Mark, as usual, got his satisfaction out of it. He preened himself on his judgment of character in having chosen me and not Philip twelve years before!

"Later on I apologized to Mark for the reckless things I had said to him, and he played the part of a magnanimous gentleman with his accustomed skill, but, though outwardly we were as before to each other, from that day forward, though his vanity would never let him see it, I was his bitterest enemy. If that had been all, I wonder if I should have killed him? To live on terms of intimate friendship with a man whom you hate is dangerous work for your friend. Because of his belief in me as his admiring and grateful protégé, and his belief in himself as my benefactor, he was now utterly in my power. I could take my time and choose my opportunity. Perhaps I should not have killed him, but I had sworn to have my revenge—and there he was, poor vain fool, at my mercy. I was in no hurry.

"Two years later I had to reconsider my position, for my revenge was being taken out of my hands. Mark began to drink. Could I have stopped him? I don't think so, but to my immense surprise I found myself trying to. Instinct, perhaps, getting the better of reason; or did I reason it out and tell myself that, if he drank himself to death, I should lose my revenge? Upon my word, I cannot tell you; but, for whatever motive, I did genuinely want to stop it. Drinking is such a beastly thing, anyhow.

"I could not stop him, but I kept him within certain bounds, so that nobody but myself knew his secret. Yes, I kept him outwardly decent; and perhaps now I was becoming like the cannibal who keeps his victim in good condition for his own ends. I used to gloat over Mark, thinking how utterly he was mine to ruin as I pleased, financially, morally, whatever way would give me most satisfaction. I had but to take my hand away from him and he sank. But again I was in no hurry.

"Then he killed himself. That futile little drunkard, eaten up with his own selfishness and vanity, offered his beastliness to the truest and purest woman on this earth. You have seen her, Mr. Gillingham, but you never knew Mark Ablett. Even if he had not been a drunkard, there was no chance for her of happiness with him. I had known him for many years, but never once had I seen him moved by any generous emotion. To have lived with that shrivelled little soul would have been hell for her; and a thousand times worse hell when he began to drink.

"So he had to be killed. I was the only one left to protect her, for her mother was in league with Mark to bring about her ruin. I would have shot him openly for her sake, and with what gladness, but I had no mind to sacrifice myself needlessly. He was in my power; I could persuade him to almost anything by flattery; surely it would not be difficult to give his death the appearance of an accident.

"I need not take up your time by telling you of the many plans I made and rejected. For some days I inclined towards an unfortunate boating accident in the pond—Mark a very indifferent swimmer, myself almost exhausted in a gallant attempt to hold him up. And then he himself gave me the idea, he and Miss Norris between them, and so put himself in my hands; without risk of discovery, I should have said, had you not discovered me.

"We were talking about ghosts. Mark had been even more vain, pompous and absurd than usual, and I could see that Miss Norris was irritated by it.

After dinner she suggested dressing up as a ghost and frightening him. I thought it my duty to warn her that Mark took any joke against himself badly, but she was determined to do it. I gave way with apparent reluctance. Reluctantly, also, I told her the secret of the passage. (There is an underground passage from the library to the bowling-green. You should exercise your ingenuity, Mr. Gillingham, in trying to discover it. Mark came upon it by accident a year ago. It was a godsend to him; he could drink there in greater secrecy. But he had to tell me about it. He wanted an audience, even for his vices.)

"I told Miss Norris, then, because it was necessary for my plan that Mark should be thoroughly frightened. Without the passage she could never have got close enough to the bowling-green to alarm him properly, but as I arranged it with her she made the most effective appearance, and Mark was in just the state of rage and vindictiveness which I required. Miss Norris, you understand, is a professional actress. I need not say that to her I appeared to be animated by no other feeling than a boyish desire to bring off a good joke—a joke directed as much against the others as against Mark.

"He came to me that night, as I expected, still quivering with indignation. Miss Norris must never be asked to the house again; I was to make a special note of it; never again. It was outrageous. Had he not a reputation as a host to keep up, he would pack her off next morning. As it was, she could stay; hospitality demanded it; but never again would she come to the Red House—he was absolutely determined about that. I was to make a special note of it.

"I comforted him, I smoothed down his ruffled feathers. She had behaved very badly, but he was

quite right; he must try not to show how much he
disapproved of her. And of course she would never
come again—that was obvious. And then suddenly I
began to laugh. He looked up at me indignantly.

" 'Is there a joke?' he said coldly.

"I laughed gently again.

" 'I was just thinking,' I said, 'that it would be
rather amusing if you—well, had your revenge.'

" 'My revenge? How do you mean?'

" 'Well, paid her back in her own coin.'

" 'Do you mean try and frighten her?'

" 'No, no; but dressed up and pulled her leg a bit.
Made her look a fool in front of the others.' I laughed
to myself again. 'Serve her jolly well right.'

"He jumped up excitedly.

" 'By Jove, Cay!' he cried. 'If I could! How? You
must think of a way.'

"I don't know if Beverley has told you about
Mark's acting. He was an amateur of all the arts, and
vain of his little talents, but as an actor he seemed
to himself most wonderful. Certainly he had some
ability for the stage, so long as he had the stage to
himself and was playing to an admiring audience.
As a professional actor in a small part he would have
been hopeless; as an amateur playing the leading
part, he deserved all that the local papers had ever
said about him. And so the idea of giving us a
private performance, directed against a professional
actress who had made fun of him, appealed equally
to his vanity and his desire for retaliation. If he,
Mark Ablett, by his wonderful acting could make
Ruth Norris look a fool in front of the others, could
take her in, and then join in the laugh at her afterwards, he would indeed have had a worthy revenge!

"(It strikes you as childish, Mr. Gillingham? Ah, you never knew Mark Ablett.)

"'How, Cay, how?' he said eagerly.

"'Well, I haven't really thought it out,' I protested. 'It was just an idea.'

"He began to think it out for himself.

"'I might pretend to be a manager, come down to see her—but I suppose she knows them all. What about an interviewer?'

"'It's going to be difficult,' I said thoughtfully. 'You've got rather a characteristic face, you know. And your beard——'

"'I'd shave it off,' he snapped.

"'My dear Mark!'

"He looked away, and mumbled, 'I've been thinking of taking it off, anyhow. And besides, if I'm going to do the thing, I'm going to do it properly.'

"'Yes, you always were an artist,' I said looking at him admiringly.

"He purred. To be called an artist was what he longed for most. Now I knew that I had him.

"'All the same,' I went on, 'even without your beard and moustache you might be recognizable. Unless, of course——' I broke off.

"'Unless what?'

"'You pretend to be Robert.' I began to laugh to myself again. 'By Jove!' I said, 'that's not a bad idea. Pretend to be Robert, the wastrel brother, and make yourself objectionable to Miss Norris. Borrow money from her, and that sort of thing.'

"He looked at me, with his bright little eyes, nodding eagerly.

"'Robert,' he said. 'Yes. How shall we work it?'

"There was really a Robert, Mr. Gillingham, as

I have no doubt you and the inspector both discovered. And he was a wastrel and he went to Australia. But he never came to the Red House on Tuesday afternoon. He couldn't have, because he died (unlamented) three years ago. But there was nobody who knew this, save Mark and myself, for Mark was the only one of the family left, and Robert had never been talked about.

"For the next two days Mark and I worked out our plans. You understand by now that our aims were not identical. Mark's endeavour was that his deception should last for, say, a couple of hours; mine that it should go to the grave with him. He had only to deceive Miss Norris and the other guests; I had to deceive the world. When he was dressed up as Robert, I was going to kill him. Robert would then be dead, Mark (of course) missing. What could anybody think but that Mark had killed Robert? But you see how important it was for Mark to enter fully into his latest (and last) impersonation. Half-measures would be fatal.

"You will say that it was impossible to do the thing thoroughly enough. I answer again that you never knew Mark. He was being what he wished most to be—an artist. No Othello ever blacked himself all over with such enthusiasm as did Mark. His beard was going anyhow—possibly a chance remark of Miss Norbury's helped here. She did not like beards. But it was important for me that the dead man's hands should not be the hands of a manicured gentleman. Five minutes playing upon the vanity of the artist settled his hands. He let the nails grow and then cut them raggedly. 'Miss Norris would notice your hands at once,' I had said. 'Besides, as an artist——'

"So with his underclothes. It was hardly necessary

to warn him that his pants might show above the edge of his socks; as an artist he had already decided upon Robertian pants. I bought them, and other things, in London for him. Even if I had not cut out all trace of the maker's name, he would instinctively have done it. As an Australian and an artist, he could not have an East London address on his underclothes. Yes, we were doing the thing thoroughly, both of us; he as an artist, I as a—well, you may say murderer, if you like. I shall not mind now.

"Our plans were settled. I went to London on the Monday and wrote him a letter from Robert. (The artistic touch again.) I also bought a revolver. On the Tuesday morning he announced the arrival of Robert at the breakfast-table. Robert was now alive—we had six witnesses to prove it; six witnesses who knew that he was coming that afternoon. Our private plan was that Robert should present himself at three o'clock, in readiness for the return of the golfing-party shortly afterwards. The maid would go to look for Mark, and having failed to find him, come back to the office to find me entertaining Robert in Mark's absence. I would explain that Mark must have gone out somewhere, and would introduce the wastrel brother to the tea-table. Mark's absence would not excite any comment, for it would be generally felt—indeed Robert would suggest it—that he had been afraid of meeting his brother. Then Robert would make himself amusingly offensive to the guests, particularly, of course, Miss Norris, until he thought that the joke had gone far enough.

"That was our private plan. Perhaps I should say that it was Mark's private plan. My own was different.

"The announcement at breakfast went well. After

the golfing-party had gone off, we had the morning in which to complete our arrangements. What I was chiefly concerned about was to establish as completely as possible the identity of Robert. For this reason I suggested to Mark that, when dressed, he should go out by the secret passage to the bowling-green, and come back by the drive, taking care to enter into conversation with the lodge-keeper. In this way I would have two more witnesses of Robert's arrival— first the lodge-keeper, and secondly one of the gardeners whom I would have working on the front lawn. Mark, of course, was willing enough. He could practise his Australian accent on the lodge-keeper. It was really amusing to see how readily he fell into every suggestion which I made. Never was a killing more carefully planned by its victim.

"He changed into Robert's clothes in the office bedroom. This was the safest way—for both of us. When he was ready, he called me in, and I inspected him. It was extraordinary how well he looked the part. I suppose that the signs of his dissipation had already marked themselves on his face, but had been concealed hitherto by his moustache and beard; for now that he was clean-shaven they lay open to the world from which we had so carefully hidden them, and he was indeed the wastrel which he was pretending to be.

" 'By Jove, you're wonderful,' I said.

"He smirked, and called my attention to the various artistic touches which I might have missed.

" 'Wonderful,' I said to myself again. 'Nobody could possibly guess.'

"I peered into the hall. It was empty. He hurried across to the library; he got into the passage and made off. I went back to the bedroom, collected all his discarded clothes, did them up in a bundle and returned with them to the passage. Then I sat down in the hall and waited.

"You heard the evidence of Stevens, the maid. As soon as she was on her way to the Temple in search of Mark, I stepped into the office. My hand was in my side-pocket, and in my hand was the revolver.

"He began at once in his character of Robert—some rigmarole about working his passage over from Australia; a little private performance for my edification. Then in his natural voice, gloating over his well-planned retaliation on Miss Norris, he burst out, 'It's my turn now. You wait.' It was this which Elsie heard. She had no business to be there and she might have ruined everything, but as it turned out it was the luckiest thing which could have happened. For it was the one piece of evidence which I wanted; evidence, other than my own, that Mark and Robert were in the room together.

"I said nothing. I was not going to take the risk of being heard to speak in that room. I just smiled at the poor little fool, and took out my revolver, and shot him. Then I went back into the library and waited—just as I said in my evidence.

"Can you imagine, Mr. Gillingham, the shock which your sudden appearance gave me? Can you imagine the feelings of a 'murderer' who has (as he thinks) planned for every possibility, and is then confronted suddenly with an utterly new problem? What difference would your coming make? I didn't know. Perhaps none; perhaps all. And I had forgotten to open the window!

"I don't know whether you will think my plan for killing Mark a clever one. Perhaps not. But if I do deserve any praise in the matter, I think I deserve it for the way I pulled myself together in the face of the unexpected catastrophe of your arrival. Yes, I got a window open, Mr. Gillingham, under your very nose; the right window too, you were kind enough to say. And the keys—yes, that was clever of you, but I think I was cleverer. I deceived you over the keys, Mr. Gillingham, as I learnt when I took the liberty of listening to a conversation on the bowling-green between you and your friend Beverley? Where was I? Ah, you must have a look for that secret passage, Mr. Gillingham.

"But what was I saying? Did I deceive you at all? You have found out the secret—that Robert was Mark —and that is all that matters. How have you found out? I shall never know now. Where did I go wrong? Perhaps you have been deceiving *me* all the time. Perhaps you knew about the keys, about the window, even about the secret passage. You are a clever man, Mr. Gillingham.

"I had Mark's clothes on my hands. I might have left them in the passage, but the secret of the passage was now out. Miss Norris knew it. That was the weak point of my plan, perhaps, that Miss Norris had to know it. So I hid them in the pond, the inspector having obligingly dragged it for me first. A couple of keys joined them, but I kept the revolver. Fortunate, wasn't it, Mr. Gillingham?

"I don't think that there is any more to tell you. This is a long letter, but then it is the last which I shall write. There was a time when I hoped that there might be a happy future for me, not at the Red House, not alone. Perhaps it was never more than an idle day-dream, for I am no more worthy of her than Mark was. But I could have made her happy, Mr. Gillingham. God, how I would have worked to make her happy! But now that is impossible. To offer her the hand of a murderer would be as bad as to offer the hand of a drunkard. And Mark died for that. I saw her this morning. She was very sweet. It is a difficult world to understand.

"Well, well, we are all gone now—the Abletts and the Cayleys. I wonder what old Grandfather Cayley thinks of it all. Perhaps it is as well that we have died out. Not that there was anything wrong with Sarah—except her temper. And she had the Ablett nose—you can't do much with that. I'm glad she left no children.

"Good-bye, Mr. Gillingham. I'm sorry that your stay with us was not of a pleasanter nature, but you understand the difficulties in which I was placed. Don't let Bill think too badly of me. He is a good fellow; look after him. He will be surprised. The young are always surprised. And thank you for letting me end my own way. I expect you did sympathize a little, you know. We might have been friends in another world—you and I, and I and she. Tell her what you like. Everything or nothing. You will know what is best. Good-bye, Mr. Gillingham.

"MATTHEW CAYLEY.

"I am lonely to-night without Mark. That's funny, isn't it?"

CHAPTER XXII

MR. BEVERLEY MOVES ON

"Good Lord!" said Bill, as he put down the letter.

"I thought you'd say that," murmured Antony.

"Tony, do you mean to say that you knew all this?"

"I guessed some of it. I didn't quite know all of it, of course."

"Good Lord!" said Bill again, and returned to the letter. In a moment he was looking up again. "What did you write to him? Was that last night? After I'd gone into Stanton?"

"Yes."

"What did you say? That you'd discovered that Mark was Robert?"

"Yes. At least I said that this morning I should probably telegraph to Mr. Cartwright of Wimpole Street, and ask him to——"

Bill burst in eagerly on the top of the sentence.

"Yes, now, what was all that about? You were so damn Sherlocky yesterday all of a sudden. We'd been doing the thing together all the time, and you'd been telling me everything, and then suddenly you become very mysterious and private and talk enigmatically—is that the word—about dentists and swimming and the 'Plough and Horses,' and—well, what was it all about? You simply vanished out of sight; I didn't know what on earth we were talking about."

Antony laughed and apologized.

"Sorry, Bill. I felt like that suddenly. Just for the last half-hour; just to end up with. I'll tell you everything now. Not that there's anything to tell, really. It seems so easy when you know it—so obvious. About Mr. Cartwright of Wimpole Street. Of course he was just to identify the body."

"But whatever made you think of a dentist for that?"

"Who could do it better? Could *you* have done it? How could you? You'd never gone bathing with Mark; you'd never seen him stripped. He didn't swim. Could his doctor do it? Not unless he'd had some particular operation, and perhaps not then. But his dentist could—at any time, always—if he had been to his dentist fairly often. Hence Mr. Cartwright of Wimpole Street."

Bill nodded thoughtfully and went back again to the letter.

"I see. And you told Cayley that you were telegraphing to Cartwright to identify the body?"

"Yes. And then of course it was all up for him. Once we knew that Robert was Mark we knew everything."

"How *did* you know?"

Antony got up from the breakfast table and began to fill his pipe.

"I'm not sure that I can say. You know those problems in Algebra where you say, 'Let *x* be the answer,' and then you work it out and find what *x* is. Well, that's one way; and another way, which they never give you any marks for at school, is to guess the answer. Guess the answer to be 4——does that satisfy all the conditions of the problem? No. Then try 6; and if 6 doesn't either, then what about 5?—and so on.

Well, the Inspector and the Coroner and all that lot
had guessed their answers, and it seemed to fit, but
you and I knew it didn't really fit; there were several
conditions in the problem which it didn't fit at all.
So we knew that their answer was wrong, and we had
to think of another—an answer which explained all
the things which were puzzling us. Well, I happened
to guess the right one. Got a match?"

Bill handed him a box, and he lit his pipe.

"Yes, but that doesn't quite do, old boy. Something must have put you on to it suddenly. By the
way, I'll have my matches back, if you don't mind."

Antony laughed and took them out of his pocket.

"Sorry. . . . Well then, let's see if I can go through
my own mind again, and tell you how I guessed it.
First of all, the clothes."

"Yes?"

"To Cayley the clothes seemed an enormously important clue. I didn't quite see why, but I did realize
that to a man in Cayley's position the smallest clue
would have an entirely disproportionate value. For
some reason, then, Cayley attached this exaggerated
importance to the clothes which Mark was wearing
on that Tuesday morning; all the clothes, the inside
ones as well as the outside ones. I didn't know why,
but I did feel certain that, in that case, the absence
of the collar was unintentional. In collecting the
clothes he had overlooked the collar. Why?"

"It was the one in the linen-basket?"

"Yes. It seemed probable. Why had Cayley put it
there? The obvious answer was that he hadn't. Mark
had put it there. I remember what you told me about
Mark being finicky, and having lots of clothes and
so on, and I felt that he was just the sort of man
who would never wear the same collar twice." He

paused, and then asked, "Is that right, do you think?"

"Absolutely," said Bill with conviction.

"Well, I guessed it was. So then I began to see an *x* which would fit just this part of the problem—the clothes part. I saw Mark changing his clothes; I saw him instinctively dropping the collar in the linen-basket, just as he had always dropped every collar he had ever taken off, but leaving the rest of the clothes on a chair in the ordinary way; and I saw Cayley collecting all the clothes afterwards—all the visible clothes—and not realizing that the collar wasn't there."

"Go on," said Bill eagerly.

"Well, I felt pretty sure about that, and I wanted an explanation of it. Why had Mark changed down there instead of in his bedroom? The only answer was that the fact of his changing had to be kept secret. When did he change? The only possible time was between lunch (when he would be seen by the servants) and the moment of Robert's arrival. And when did Cayley collect the clothes in a bundle? Again, the only answer was 'Before Robert's arrival.' So another *x* was wanted—to fit those three conditions."

"And the answer was that a murder was intended, even before Robert arrived?"

"Yes. Well now, it couldn't be intended on the strength of that letter, unless there was very much more behind the letter than we knew. Nor was it possible a murder could be intended without any more preparation than the changing into a different suit in which to escape. The thing was too childish. Also, if Robert was to be murdered, why go out of the way to announce his existence to you all—even, at the cost of some trouble, to Mrs. Norbury? What did it all mean? I didn't know. But I began to feel now that Robert was an incident only; that the plot was a plot of Cayley's against Mark—either to get him to kill his brother, or to get his brother to kill him—and that for some inexplicable reason Mark seemed to be lending himself to the plot." He was silent for a little, and then said, almost to himself, "I had seen the empty brandy bottles in that cupboard."

"You never said anything about them," complained Bill.

"I only saw them afterwards. I was looking for the collar, you remember. They came back to me afterwards; I knew how Cayley would feel about it. . . . Poor devil!"

"Go on," said Bill.

"Well, then, we had the inquest, and of course I noticed, and I suppose you did too, the curious fact that Robert had asked his way at the second lodge and not at the first. So I talked to Amos and Parsons. That made it more curious. Amos told me that Robert had gone out of his way to speak to him; had called to him, in fact. Parsons told me that his wife was out in their little garden at the first lodge all the afternoon, and was certain that Robert had never come past it. He also told me that Cayley had put him on to a job on the front lawn that afternoon. So I had another guess. Robert had used the secret passage—the passage which comes out into the park between the first and second lodges. Robert, then, had been in the house; it was a put-up job between Robert and Cayley. But how could Robert be there without Mark knowing? Obviously, Mark knew too. What did it all mean?"

"When was this?" interrupted Bill. "Just after the inquest—after you'd seen Amos and Parsons, of course!"

"Yes. I got up and left them, and came to look for

you. I'd got back to the clothes then. Why did Mark change his clothes so secretly? Disguise? But then what about his face? That was much more important than clothes. His face, his beard—he'd have to shave off his beard—and then—oh, idiot! I saw you looking at that poster. Mark acting, Mark made-up, Mark disguised. Oh, priceless idiot! Mark was Robert. . . . Matches, please."

Bill passed over the matches again, waited till Antony had relit his pipe, and then held out his hand for them, just as they were going into the other's pocket.

"Yes," said Bill thoughtfully. "Yes. . . . But wait a moment. What about the 'Plough and Horses'?"

Antony looked comically at him.

"You'll never forgive me, Bill," he said. "You'll never come clue-hunting with me again."

"What do you mean?"

Antony sighed.

"It was a fake, Watson. I wanted you out of the way. I wanted to be alone. I'd guessed at my *x*, and I wanted to test it—to test it every way, by everything we'd discovered. I simply *had* to be alone just then. So——" he smiled and added, "Well, I knew you wanted a drink."

"You *are* a devil," said Bill, staring at him. "And your interest when I told you that a woman had been staying there——"

"Well, it was only polite to be interested when you'd taken so much trouble."

"You brute! You—you Sherlock! And then you keep trying to steal my matches. Well, go on."

"That's all. My *x* fitted."

"Did you guess Miss Norris and all that?"

"Well, not quite. I didn't realize that Cayley had worked for it from the beginning—had put Miss Norris up to frightening Mark. I thought he'd just seized the opportunity."

Bill was silent for a long time. Then, puffing at his pipe, he said slowly, "Has Cayley shot himself?"

Antony shrugged his shoulders.

"Poor devil," said Bill. "It was decent of you to give him a chance. I'm glad you did."

"I couldn't help liking Cayley in a kind of way, you know."

"He's a clever devil. If you hadn't turned up just when you did, he would never have been found out."

"I wonder. It was ingenious, but it's often the ingenious thing which gets found out. The awkward thing from Cayley's point of view was that, though Mark was missing, neither he nor his body could ever be found. Well, that doesn't often happen with a missing man. He generally gets discovered in the end; a professional criminal, perhaps not—but an amateur like Mark! He might have kept the secret of *how* he killed Mark, but I think it would have become obvious sooner or later that he *had* killed him."

"Yes, there's something in that. . . . Oh, just tell me one thing. Why did Mark tell Miss Norbury about his imaginary brother?"

"That's puzzled me rather, too. it may be that he was just doing the Othello business—painting himself black all over. I mean he may have been so full of his appearance as Robert that he had almost got to believe in Robert, and had to tell everybody. More likely, though, he felt that, having told all of you at the house, he had better tell Mrs. Norbury, in case she met one of you; in which case, if you mentioned the approaching arrival of Robert, she might say, 'Oh, I'm certain he has no brother; he would have told me if he had,' and so spoil his joke. Possibly, too,

Cayley put him on to it; Cayley obviously wanted as many people as possible to know about Robert."

"Are you going to tell the police?"

"Yes, I suppose they'll have to know. Cayley may have left another confession. I hope he won't give me away; you see, I've been a sort of accessory since yesterday evening. And I must go and see Miss Norbury."

"I asked," explained Bill, "because I was wondering what I should say to—to Betty. Miss Calladine. You see, she's bound to ask."

"Perhaps you won't see her again for a long time," said Antony sadly.

"As a matter of fact, I happen to know that she will be at the Barringtons. And I go up there tomorrow."

"Well, you had better tell her. You're obviously longing to. Only don't let her say anything for a day or two. I'll write to you."

"Righto!"

Antony knocked the ashes out of his pipe and got up.

"The Barringtons," he said. "Large party?"

"Fairly, I think."

Antony smiled at his friend.

"Yes. Well, if any of them *should* happen to be murdered, you might send for me. I'm just getting into the swing of it."